'A quirky but fascinating novel which, presented as a letter from a father to his daughter, covers serious philosophical and existential issues through parables and Vedantic reflections.'

Dr Karan Singh
Chairman of the Auroville Foundation, politician, philanthropist, and poet

'A brilliant and original novel by Shubhrangshu Roy, *Zara's Witness* uses fantasy, myth, science, music, poetry, and stream of consciousness to communicate deep insights on the nature of inner reality. Zara begins her journey up in the mountains and by the river. She wonders who she is, and she is taught by creatures of the forest – a frog, a lizard, an elephant, a hyena, and a turtle – the elements, and the river. She confronts questions of being and identity and learns that willing renunciation is the essence of bliss. The book is like a prose-poem that asks to be read and re-read, while nudging the reader to mystical truths.'

Dr Subhash Kak
Author, Vedic scholar, professor of artificial intelligence and on the Indian prime minister's advisory council on science, technology, and innovation

'Shubhrangshu Roy's groundbreaking *Zara's Witness* has rightly been called "brilliant and original" by Dr Subhash Kak—researcher, scholar, author, professor, and world authority on Indo-European studies and Information Science. In impact, *Zara* will smile in the company of

contd ...

Bach's *Jonathan Livingstone Seagull*, Saint-Exupéry's *The Little Prince*, Gibran's *The Prophet*, and Coelho's *The Alchemist*. After the ersatz blossoming of Mahesh Yogi and Ravi Shankar nudged by the Beatles' self-grafting, this is a breath of fresh air blown from India's multi-millennial civilisation. It tests the reader's focus and throws a challenge to finish it and titillates dormant mechanisms fretting over the essentials of Being.'

Prof Azam Gill
Author

'If you were to make a cocktail of Jostein Gaarder's *Sophie's World*, mix in Robert Pirsig's *Zen and the Art of Motorcycle Maintenance*, lace it with generous measure of Indic philosophy and metaphysics, and garnish the whole with a slice of Joycean stream-of-consciousness, you might come up with an approximation of *Zara's Witness*. *Zara's Witness* deserves not just to be read but to be listened to, fully to realise the multi-layered message and meaning it seeks to convey?

Are you ready to listen?'

Jug Suraiya in The Speaking Tree

'I'm very impressed. My impression is that he has written this book for a market who have both a spiritual inquisitiveness (at least) and those who love the idea of escapism for a period of time into another realm. I think he has achieved this.'

Annie De Monchaux
Author

'For Shubhrangshu Roy, the nature of Indian philosophy and the diverse aspirations of it not only spirals upwards, i.e., it ascends from one story to another, but it is also essentially recursive. Which is to say, it is never-ending and almost amounts to the same thing being told over and over again through shifts in the storytelling from generation to generation, from one millennium to another. In a sense, there is actually no ending, no conclusion. The storyteller and the story can go on and on. This reminds us of the never-ending story of the German writer Michael Ende, who has written a similar story for children and teens. As a never-ending story, the narrator becomes part of the story and the differences between the story and the hero become indistinguishable. Here the individual self, liberated from the illusion of identity, follows the cycles of life, death, and rebirth together with the whole cosmic processes.'

Father Kuruvilla Pandikattu, SJ
Professor of Philosophy at Jnana Deepa Papal Seminary, Pune

'Well, this is a different narrative. A letter from a father to his daughter on the meaning of freedom, becoming, nature, and refusing to succumb to the obsessive cycles of unfreedoms. This book is an ode to her liberation, her freedom, the wind in her hair, the salt in the air, the gleam in her eyes. A beautiful philosophical tribute, which is not an escape, but a miracle waiting to happen, like magic.'

Amit Sengupta in *HNFP.in*

'A marvellous story, full of the joy of life!'

John K Lewis
Former co-founder at Consolidated Technologies and scholar of theoretical physics from RU Utrecht.

'I enjoyed the book. So many beautiful philosophies, metaphors, and analogies about the journey of life. I would pursue this book. I loved what Shubhrangshu had to say.'

Jane Haybittel
Author and businesswoman

'AMAZING. Master stylist. Enjoying every twirl and turn of words and thoughts. The expressive language is unmatched.'

Amita Sharma
Former additional secretary,
Ministry of Human Resources
Development and architect of the MNREGA initiative

'*Zara's Witness* is bursting with vivid descriptions of nature; the central character is schooled by forces of nature like the frog, lizard, elephant, hyena et al.'

Sneha Bhura in *The Week*

'An absurdly fabulous book of brilliant writing: The author has done one hell of a crazy bit of writing that takes you to spaces from mythology to science to music with absolute ease, pretty much sharing his own interests in three different areas.'

Sharif Rangnekar
Festival director of Rainbow Lit Fest and author of *Straight to Normal*

'Presented as a letter from a father to a daughter, it is not the usual bunch of homilies that daddy hands out to his little girl. Instead, this original novel uses fantasy, myth, science, music and poetry, and stream of consciousness to communicate deep insights of the nature of inner reality.'

Ranjit Bhushan in *DNA*

'Hop on, it's a journey worth taking. Roy has taken a complicated idea that had our ancient sages delving into their minds for eons—who am I—and has made it into an adventure. A beautiful read that takes us on a journey that for some could only be described as spiritual.'

Jemima Raman
Book critic at *The Times of India*

'This book is aimed towards anyone who is trying to find their purpose in life. After a lot of days, I was able to read something miraculous and beautiful. This book focuses on self-discovery and the challenges which one faces during a lifetime. The author's writing is so beautiful and philosophical that it will definitely connect with an avid reader easily. It has a beautiful cover as well and I will recommend it to everyone.'

Rujuta Ramteke
Book critic and social media influencer

ZARA'S WITNESS

A Soul Journey into the Nature of Being

Shubhrangshu Roy

Hay House Publishers India
Australia • India
United Kingdom • United States

Hay House Publishers (India) Pvt. Ltd.
Muskaan Complex, Plot No.3, B-2 Vasant Kunj, New Delhi-110 070, India
Hay House Inc., PO Box 5100, Carlsbad, CA 92018-5100, USA
Hay House UK, Ltd., The Sixth Floor, Watson House, 54 Baker Street, W1U 7BU, UK
Hay House Australia Pty Ltd., 18/36 Ralph St., Alexandria NSW 2015, Australia
Email: contact@hayhouse.co.in
www.hayhouse.co.in

First reprint 2022

shubhrangshu.roy@gmail.com
shubhrangshuroy.com

ISBN 978- 93-86832-89-4
ISBN 978-93-86832-90-0 (e-book)

Printed at Repro India Limited

To the one within

Contents

Level V
The End of Story: The Game Begins

Appendices

Introduction

Dear Zara,

This book is for you, but it's not your story.

It is more of a coming-of-age manual for you as you step into your teens today.

Zara's Witness is a philosophical fantasy capturing the journey of a girl—from infancy to adulthood—in search of an answer to that eternal human question: who am I? That search meanders along the course of a river to its final destination in the sky where both the river and the human spirit merge at the end of the journey to discover the one eternal truth revealed to mankind since time immemorial—universal love.

The book has been scripted since you were one year old and is based on conversations with one of India's least publicised masters of a spiritual cult—that has some of India's wealthiest citizens among its select followers—at the foot of the Himalayas. In *Zara's Witness*, the pupil becomes the infant girl, Zara, journeying to her destination along the course of the Ganges. The Master becomes the river.

The book combines the wisdom of the spiritual master with over 5,000 years of Vedic expositions in a series of hallucinatory journeys that deliver the core of Indian philosophy in a little over 35,000 words of adventure-driven drama in primordial, contemporary, and futuristic settings.

Reader: Zara's Witness is primarily aimed at you, the young-adult reader, to introduce you to Indian spiritual wisdom in an age that is widely believed will usher in the return to Indic knowledge traditions for balanced global development. At yet another level, it is also aimed to arouse the aesthete in you so that you may grow up to be well-versed in the best universal values and appreciate the finer nuances of life.

Technique: According to noted Indologist Wendy Doniger's book, *The Hindus: An Alternative History*, the conversation is the centrepiece of the book, for which, the narration is merely a frame. The book deploys several tools used in other crafts and science such as literature, poetry, theatre, classical Indian and Western music, cinema, and quantum computing to narrate Zara's inner exploration.

It uses jump cuts, techniques of landscape painting, elements of magic realism, jungle adventure, theatrical and musical extravaganza, and culinary craft to tell the story. It also draws on the technique of *alaap** in classical Indian music and the concept of arias and libretto in classical Western opera, in order to reach crescendo in rapid bursts, before culminating in rapture.

*Alaap is the improvised section of a raga, forming a prologue to the formal expression.

Adapting influences from classical Indian texts, the first three sections of the book—Level I through Level III—serve as the *purva paksha**, narrating what the masters have said and say to this day. The last two sections—Level IV and Level V—draw on the deeper mysteries of the Universe expounded in the age-old texts to leap forward and illustrate a robust, contemporary philosophy. It is here that *shlokas* from the English renditions of the Upanishads by Indic scholars, S Radhakrishnan and Eknath Easwaran, have been woven into the narrative in Zara's final conversations with her higher self before she ascends to the sky to confront the one and only reality of her being—I am who thou art, thou art who I am—rendered eloquently in our mystic traditions as *Aham Brahmasmi, Tat Tvam Asi.*

A final section, an after-conversation, is a copyright blueprint of the 'equation for everything in the Universe' articulated as 'the essence of this and that'. You will find this equation interspersed throughout the narrative. The concept of time and space, as measured by ancient seers, is elaborated at the end of the book. It has been used to map age and distances in the story.

Hope you enjoy reading this book in your journey through life.

Happy Birthday!
Dad

*Purva paksha is a tradition in *dharma* discourse which involves building a deep familiarity with the opponent's point of view before criticising it.

Level I

The Song of Creation

Chapter 1

Zara woke up to the first flush of light, peering out of the giant plasma bubble, as she lay damp, cradled in the wedge between the rock and the nine rock steps to the river on its eastern flank. It was early autumn. The night sky was giving way to the ochre rays of the sun over the eastern horizon from behind the Peacock Ridge.

The western sky was still dark as the moon prepared to take its last bow behind the Moonshine Mount—so called because of the massive crest of snow atop a giant black granite that glowed in the radiance of the full moon, its feet skirted by the pink sandstone Ah!nandita Hills, kissed by nine similar steps climbing the far bank of the river.

The barren rock was too steep and too foreboding for humans to set foot on. Folklore had it that whoever climbed the rock and reached the snow-white peak would ride off to paradise where no human mind had ventured before.

Since time immemorial, that folklore had been a great temptation for mind adventurers and, yet, a great deterrent. So, they let the mountain be. For no one dare tread its uncharted path for fear of what might lie ahead.

It had been a different story with the mountain to the east, however, that stood a fair distance from the riverbank. Everybody came to the river from far beyond the Peacock Ridge—that glistened in the dazzle of massive gemstones that lighted up its crest by night—where the glamour of human mind revelled in the great metropolis, rolling the dice since the dawn of civilisation in hope and joy, fame and fortune, celebration and euphoria, rubbing shoulders with dejection and despair, fear and sorrow, and squalor and agony.

And so, it was from beyond the Peacock Ridge that countless souls found their way to the river, down the ages, and across age groups, in search of an answer to that eternal existential question in the mind of every living and in the memory of every dead who had left their calling card behind. And that question repeated itself in three simple words:

Who . . . am . . . I?

And with the eternal flow of that question, the river, too, flowed forever as the great divide between the dazzle of the body (as represented by the Peacock Ridge) and the barrenness of the soul (as represented by the Moonshine Mount).

It had been one long journey for Zara till she had got stuck on the wedge. No one quite knew exactly when she came to be perched here, in the cover of dark, to be eventually delivered.

And now, as the orange ball of fire rose to the east

above the ridge, Zara lay warming in her bubble, looking up at the mellow early morning sky in wonderment. It had only been a while since she had let out a shrill cry of panic as the long dark shadow of fear crossed her face at the first wink of the light. Soon, however, that frown was replaced by a bewildered smile at the pleasant glow of dawn.

From where she lay, head south, Zara turned her face to the left, catching the flight of an unending flock of tittiri birds, sending ripples of their shadows across the river face below the Ah!nandita Hills. Zara laughed, turned skywards, looked west again, and laughed louder; she looked straight up to the sky, turned right to the sun in the eastern sky, and laughed still louder as the wind picked up her mirth and flew off towards the flight path of the tittiris heading north, the fading ripples of her laughter echoed across the sky. And those ripples mingled with the clang of a thousand bells that now rent the air.

And Zara's mind raced back to where she belonged.

Zara's story was scripted first at the bottom of the glacier, at the head of the river, high up in the mountains, where, across a desolate landscape lay countless plasma bubbles, one heaped upon the other, one beside the other, packed by the zillions in unglued bonding, in the fearful darkness before dawn. Zara, a thousand times smaller than a speck of dust, lay there among a multitude of her likeness, one of many, waiting in silent stillness. Waiting and waiting and waiting.

And then, darkness crept upon darkness in slow motion, in warm embrace, in the frozen wilderness, and high up there in the valley, emotion gave way to motion, and motion gave way to warmth, and warmth gave way to speed, and speed gave way to heat, and heat gave way to friction, and friction cracked the glacier.

That's when the tongue of the glacier rolled over, licking its own bruises from the tension of its heat, melting. Melting drop by drop in a watery trickle; and so, the bubbles drifted from their moorings and slipped out . . . one by one. Growing, growing, and growing. First, a hundred thousand times larger to the size of a tip of the human hair, and then five times as big. Speeding, riding the torrent, one colliding against another, choking each other of breath, drowning one too many, ripping each other open . . .

. . . before stillness regained control once more.

Zara's existential race had begun, among the multitude of her likeness. One of many, she alone would survive to see daybreak by the riverbank, having grown to the size of a mustard seed, round and perfect, a millimetre across.

Chapter 2

Slowly, morning gave way to noon, and noon to sundown. And the tittiris headed back to the nest as a thousand bells rose to rent the air in unison to the accompaniment of the heart-tugging blows of a thousand conch shells.

And the river came alive at dusk as a thousand upon thousands of lamps in small leaf cups floated downstream past the bubble, still perched atop the wedge into the distance, where the cows lowed, from where they ascended heavenwards.

Zara lay still. Still bewildered. Watching the day go by. Thinking deep. Taking in her surroundings in silent amusement. Till the dark night sky lit up to the glitter of the Peacock Ridge to the east and the dazzle of the snow-crested granite beyond the Ah!nandita Hills to the west.

Soon, the play of light and sound reached a crescendo, as a thousand giant glow-worms sprang up to dance on the promenade leading from the eastern steps. And one by one, one after another, one and together, they danced in night-time revelry in a psychedelic display of merriment by the river. Zara watched, watched, and watched.

And the night sky in the distance beyond the ridge glowed a thousand miles away in the neon-lit revelry of the metropolis trapped in a whirl of illusion and delusion, euphoric, celebrating hope and joy, fame and fortune, till the wee hours, before daylight ushered in dark dejection and despair in fear and sorrow of the squalor and agony of life.

Life in the metro lived by night as dozens of damsels in skintight leggings and hot pants with tank tops and off-shoulders gyrated on the floor of the neighbourhood disc—bare shoulder to bare shoulder, bum to bum, to the beat of synthetic music—cheered by the shrill whistles of countless leering bystanders, far, far away from where Zara was stationed this very moment, her life still hanging on the wedge.

And night gave way to dawn, and dawn to day, and day to dusk in an endless cycle; life went on from season to season. And Zara grew, first to the size of a grain of rice, to a barleycorn, to a thumb, a palm, a foot, and, finally, an arm's length.

And the torrential monsoon rains gave way to pleasant autumn that gave way to winter chill, and winter chill to severe cold, and severe cold to refreshing spring, and spring to scorching summer, when, suddenly, one hot morning, unpredicted by the tittiris on the western bank, the bubble ruptured, and Zara came crashing on the dry river bed strewn with rocks and pebbles.

It had been 24,192,000 seconds to the dot since she had slipped out of the glacier's tongue, 2,520 miles up north.

Jolted out of her reverie, Zara panicked and let out a primordial cry.

'Whoaaaaa . . . maaaa . . . eeeee?' Zara broke her silence, aloud, crawling, face up to the midday sun.

'Whoaaaaa . . . maaaaiii?' she cried aloud once more.

'Whoo . . . am . . . aaaii?' the wind answered as Zara's heart-rending existential cry went knocking to and fro between the Moonshine Mount and the Peacock Ridge. And the tittiri birds, which had been busy with their morning chores in the shade of the giant banyan at the foot of the Ah!nandita Hills, sprang up in a flutter, their diligence disrupted, before silence regained its creep once more.

Zara turned around towards the eastern steps on the bank.

Crawling, tumbling, creeping, and growing, when she chanced upon a monitor lizard peering from between the rocks, in silent meditation, in a handsome slant, erect from shoulder upwards, gauging the sky before its tongue darted out to chase the dragonfly hovering above; at a short distance, in a pool of still water on the dry river bed, a frog croaked aloud; a train of busy ants crawled the bed on its way to the bank. Zara looked on.

A common housefly that had all along been busy at a nearby rot suddenly appeared on the scene and squatted prettily on the tip of her nose. Zara peered down the ridge of her nose for an eye-to-eye with the fly, her bright brown pupils glaring, as a pair of huge red bulbous protrusions stared back at Zara, sending ripples down her spine.

A couple of grasshoppers had parked themselves on

the steps by now, even as a giant butterfly swooped down the bank. Zara looked up in awe. The frog croaked aloud, again, beckoning Zara to the pool. Distracted, Zara turned to her right and crawled. Turning over the rocks and pebbles that lay strewn between her and the pool. It was a while before Zara made her way to the watery patch.

Right across the pool, from where she crept, Zara looked up to a large brown pillar rising to the sky, and then another, and another two behind. A long, fat rope came hanging down from above, swaying left to right, right to left, as another rope swayed behind the rear two pillars. It was the elephant.

Her world was as much new to Zara as Zara was new to her world—the lizard, the dragonfly, the frog, the ants, the housefly, the butterfly, the grasshoppers, the elephant, and . . . Zara. Zara stared at the pool. Her mirror image from inside its glazed surface stared back at Zara. And so, Zara stared at Zara inside the pool, the overhead sun, now a tiny ball in reflection.

'Who are you?' Zara asked her image.

'Who are you?' the image asked her back.

'Who am I?' asked Zara, peering deep within into her own self and then deep outside at her image in the pool.

Ripples went out in circles on the pool's surface and then sprang up in a fountain from its centre, spraying droplets on Zara's face, drenching her all over in the midday sun, as a sing-song voice rose from deep within the bowels of the pool. 'I am Who,' came the voice.

And then, followed a sweet song, '*Jo tu hai, so main hoon; jo main hoon, so tu hai!*' (What you are, so am I; what I am, so are you!)

'Come again', Zara said to herself, stare frozen, ears erect, those magical, comforting words, incomprehensible.

'Have faith in yourself, Zara,' said the voice from within the pool. 'No one here is bigger than you, nor is anyone smaller than you are. Not the ant, not the housefly, not the butterfly, not the dragonfly, not the grasshopper, not the frog, not the monitor lizard, and, least of all, not the elephant. Come look again, little Zara, neither is there any joy for you around this place nor is there any sorrow . . . what you are, little Zara, so I am; what I am, so you are.'

And then, all fell silent.

Dazed, Zara took a while to regain her bearings before she turned to her surroundings again. The elephant, the lizard, the grasshopper, the dragonfly, the butterfly, the housefly, and the ants were all gone.

Silent, Zara raised her ears. The frog croaked once more, then, hopped out of the pool. And hop, hop, hop it went, towards the steps on the eastern bank.

It must have been a long crawl for Zara from the time her bubble burst open till her rendezvous with her self by the pool. Shrugging off her magic encounter, Zara pulled herself up. And as the frog hopped out of the pool and went off towards the steps, she turned, one faltering step at a time, in the footsteps of the frog.

Hop, hop, hop, the frog jumped, pausing at every hop, letting out a croak; its tongue darting out time and again, much like the lizard earlier, snacking on every flying worm that came its way, gluttony bloating its stomach.

Zara giggled at its sight, imitated the hop, and fell. Then, she collected herself, toddling in unbalanced gait on her tender legs over the rocks and pebbles on the river bed.

Level II

The Illusion of Identity

Chapter 1

It had started drizzling, and, soon, a steady downpour came calling from the sky as a stream appeared on the river bed, swallowing up the pool in a moment.

'Hurry,' the frog croaked at Zara, taking one last giant hop to the eastern bank and landing on all fours on the first step from the river.

Drenched all over, Zara, now a sprightly twelve-year-old, hurried as the stream rushed to her ankles.

'Hurry up!' the frog croaked again before Zara took her last faltering step to the bank.

'Whew! You made it on time,' the frog told Zara as she gasped for breath. And then, she turned back to take one long good look at the river, now in full flow by the bank.

'Hi Zara!' the frog beckoned with a smile. 'Did you notice how the pool of water recognised you when you first asked her who you were?'

Zara, amused, raised her brows and nodded, a smile smeared across her face.

'Yes, that's right. How did it happen?' she asked.

'That's magic,' said the frog. 'You remember all those creatures by the pool: the ants, the housefly, the butterfly, the dragonfly, the grasshopper, the lizard, and the elephant? They all came down to the river to quench their existential thirst. And yet, you stood out, one among many, and the river recognised who you really are.'

'That's fascinating,' Zara wondered aloud. 'How did all this happen? I had never felt so wanted before. The river gave me the comfort of my diverse surroundings—of insects, animals, and plants.' And saying so, Zara turned to the river.

'Who are you?' she asked.

The river, now in spate, laughed aloud. 'Ha! me, Zara? I am what you are. Better still, I am what you perceive I am. Right now, dear Zara, you perceive me a giant swell of water in spate, and yet, not long ago, I was only a puddle till I became a pool, a stream, a river. When I am here, as I now am, I am what you see me to be. And when I am many hundred miles down south, I am a giant ocean. But Zara, I am not just this, and this, and this, that you have seen me to be. Up there, high in the mountains where you originally belong, I was solid ice that gave shape to the glacier. And before I froze into ice, dear Zara, I was soft, woolly snow formed by droplets of water accumulated in the sky.'

'O Rivah! I can see you on the ground as a river that I have seen so far, at times a puddle, at times a pool, and now, as a massive swell. I can imagine you rushing down here in a torrent, just the way I came riding you in a bubble from high up in freezing wilderness. But, dear Rivah!, how do I ever catch you in the sky, if all you say is perception?'

'Hang on, Zara,' the river replied. 'You'll learn more as you grow. I keep changing forever as perceptions about me keep changing. So will you now that you have come down to earth.

Zara raised her brows again and asked, 'But please, Rivah! please tell me how you got to ride the sky, just as you get to ride the earth right now?'

'Oh well, Zara,' said the river, 'that's a long story. When I reach my destination and become the ocean and the world can hold me no more in the sweltering heat, I rise to the sky above, reaching out to tame the sun as cloud. But then, in the piercing cold of the sky, I long for the comforting cradle of the earth and begin to cry. And so, I descend again to earth, sometimes as rain, at times as snow, and, thus, I ride another cycle. That's life, Zara, that's your story as well as mine. It's just a change of form. It's just a change of perception.'

'Remember, jo tu hai, so main hoon; jo main hoon, so tu hai!' the river said in the now familiar sing-song voice.

And the thousand bells began to toll once more. Unnoticed by Zara, the sun had gone down behind the Moonshine Mount. The neon glaze from the metro beyond the Peacock Ridge lit up the distant sky in a soft and subdued glow. And then, the glow-worms came to life in thousands on the steps of the eastern bank, drowning Zara in a sea of twinkling lights amidst the surrounding darkness as more bells rent the air to the accompaniment of a thousand conch shells. And the lamps in leaf cups came floating down the river before rising to the sky in the distance.

Zara sat on the first step by the river, her feet dipped in the flowing water, lost deep in contemplation.

It wasn't long before darkness crept in all over again.

CHAPTER 2

Zara woke up to a scary sight at the first rays of dawn. Still sitting on the step, her feet dipped in water, her head tilted to the left, her left cheek resting on the flat of her palm; she had dozed off the night before in deep contemplation. Before long, a sudden drone broke her sleep. As if a chopper was approaching her from the rear and then, a couple . . . a dozen . . . a hundred and more . . .

Hmmmmm! came the buzz, growing louder by the second.

Zara turned back from the river to the flight of steps, climbing down from the promenade. Swarms of giant worms and little crawlies came creeping down towards the river from the rise above. Soon, every square inch of the steps was covered by creatures in green, and yellow, and black, and brown, and red, each larger than the other—ants by the billions, caterpillars, earthworms, houseflies, bees, butterflies, dragonflies, grasshoppers, frogs, and lizards. Every worm, every creature in millions after millions, in wave after wave, crawling down the steps, each little worm trying to outpace the other, pushing one to the other aside.

Soon, the sky, too, filled up with swarms clouding the Peacock Ridge and the Moonshine Mount on the bank across rising above the Ah!nandita Hills, darkening the sky in broad daylight, as the buzz grew louder and louder and louder.

'They are going to crawl all over me,' Zara shivered in panic, her peach-red face turned pale. She shut her eyes tight and tucked her face into her arms crossed over her knees, her head reeling from the buzz.

Finally, when she came around and lifted her head, it was quiet again. A sweet, musical voice loomed over her shoulder. 'Rest easy, folks. Focus within yourself. Gather your wits. It's time for lessons,' whispered the giant butterfly.

And then, she heard a domineering command, 'Do not rest your eyes on what you see around. Do not seek the external manifestation of what really is within. Seek the silence of your soul, seek the wisdom of your heart,' the monitor lizard strutted about, inspecting and instructing.

Zara looked around. The giant butterfly fluttered overhead as the rest of the creatures settled quietly on the steps, at elbow distance from Zara, sparing just enough space to turn her head around. The old and the infirm were still on the promenade, peering down at the river. The young and the agile had settled on the lower steps, next to Zara. A couple of youngsters lazed around at the top among the laggards, while a few able-bodied among the elders sat by the waterside.

Zara noticed the frog who had led her to the steps, at a distance, sitting in silent contemplation, an eye still on her, but unmindful of the creatures that would otherwise make for a feast any other time. The monitor lizard sat right behind her on the step above. Only the butterflies still fluttered, in silence, spreading radiance in the sky that looked so violently scary not so long ago. On the bank across the river, the tittiris had parked themselves in a single row on the first step from the river at the feet of the Ah!nandita Hills, pecking at the red fig seeds from the banyan tree scattered all over. Nearby, a couple of swans courted each other, as did two vain peacocks strutting from here to there, flaunting their rich, colourful plumes. A crocodile basked in the sunshine at a distance, brooding over a batch of eggs. And the river, its clear green water, flowed between the banks.

Zara looked deep into the water. Giant mahseers meditated in stillness even as the water rushed over them at high velocity.

And she rested her chin in the cusp of her palms that, in turn, rested on her elbows that rested on her thighs.

'It's so quiet and peaceful around. The creatures are so calm. Then, why the mad scramble?' Zara wondered. And she thought, and thought, and thought . . . delving deep within, when unnoticed by her, the river stopped her flow.

'Good morning, Rivah! Wish us well,' the creatures bowed, chanting aloud, together.

'Good morning! Wish you well, dear life,' the river replied. And then, rising in a gigantic wave, she sang:

I know not how to bow, O Rivah!
Please teach me how to bend.

'I know not how to bow, O Rivah! Please teach me how to bend,' all the creatures joined in chorus. And the butterflies danced, and the crickets chirped, and the dragonflies hovered their wings, and the bees buzzed aloud, and the lizards strummed air guitars, while the caterpillars and the earthworms and the rest took to the floor. From the top, on the promenade, the elephant blew his trumpet as the air filled with joy and cheer.

Zara jumped up from where she had been sitting.

'I know not how to bow, O Rivah! Please teach me how to bend,' she sang, going around in a whirl, her hands raised to shoulder height, outstretched, on the water's edge.

Chapter 3

It was a while before the whirling came to a stop and all the creatures led by Zara sat down in contemplative silence—the air still fresh, the sun up there, spreading its radiance across the whole wide world. The river, calm and still, had regained her dignified flow.

'Come one and all, it's time for a dip,' the river said to the creatures gathered on her bank. 'Come, sip the joy of life from my flowing water.'

And the creatures, in ones and twos and in groups of fives and tens, dipped into the water, dipping their heads in silence. The frog jumped in first and then, jumped out, repeating the ritual thrice over. The monitor lizard went in next, and then, the ants, the houseflies, the bees, the butterflies, the dragonflies, the grasshoppers, and, finally, the elephant, with a loud splash.

On the opposite bank, at the feet of Ah!nandita Hills, the tittiris, meditating in a single file, dipped their beaks into the water.

'Come, lemme cleanse your minds,' the river said in a dignified tone.

'For when I am one with myself within, I rid myself of the dilemmas of my mind.'

'When I am one with myself within, I rid myself of

the dilemmas of my mind,' the creatures chanted one by one with their first dip into water.

'And so, I rid myself of the dilemmas of my body,' the river chanted.

'And so, I rid myself of the dilemmas of my body,' the creatures repeated with their second dip into water.

'And so, I rid myself of the dilemmas of my belongings,' the river chanted the third time.

'And so, I rid myself of the dilemmas of my belongings,' the creatures chanted with their third dip into water.

'How do you do this?' the river asked the creatures. And they looked askance at her.

'First,' said the river, 'you strip your mind naked of all layers of thought, of all perceptions you have acquired over the years and that now belong to you. That's how you cleanse your mind.'

'O dear creatures of my Universe! Take back this knowledge when you are gone. Take it to your home, to your work, to your very own world where you belong. Get rid of the belongings of your minds, your perceptions of you and me. Give up your longings for joy, give up your sorrows. Give up your idea of who you are.'

'Give up, give up, give up!' the river went on.

'And the more you do so, the cleaner you get,' she added.

'And how does that happen?' the butterfly hissed.

'Just as gold acquires a greater halo the more you heat it on fire; it is the same with you and me. So, dip,

dip, dip. Immerse yourself. Rejig yourself first. Wash yourself clean,' the river replied.

And then, turning to the frog who had guided Zara to the bank, the river said in a grave voice, 'Wash yourself clean first before you try it out on others.'

Zara, who was by now the only creature left unwashed, rested her forehead on her left palm, immersed in her own self, thinking.

'Make the entire Universe your own. The river, the fish, the birds, the worms, the reptiles and all. And to make them your own, renounce the image you have of yourself,' the river flowed on.

'But how does one do that?' Zara got thinking.

That is when, someone hit her hard. *Tchk, tchk, tchk.* The monitor lizard knocked his knuckles on the back of her head.

Zara, as now seemed to have become a habit, had been resting her forehead on her palm, reflecting on the river, while sitting on the steps as the butterflies circled above.

'Nobody sits by the river that way,' the lizard chided Zara. 'You are supposed to sit erect, shoulder up like me, and soak the wisdom of the river, not immerse yourself in your small, silly thoughts. Sink yourself in the wisdom of the river, O Zara! Go take a jump.'

So far, Zara had been watching the river flow past, listening to whatever it said. But that was just about all. It never occurred to her that she needed to take a dip, just as the other creatures around her had been doing, chanting words of faith and self-belief with every dip.

Then, knocking its knuckles again, he mocked, 'Just look at yourself, look at your stupor, Zara. You are ageing while you are young. Come, get here,' he directed her to the step above, knocking harder, making space for her where he had been sitting all this while.

'You will hear the river better from here,' the lizard said, and disappeared to nowhere.

'What is it?' Zara asked herself. 'The monitor, it's gone. But why did he admonish me when he doesn't even know who I am?'

Zara thought, and thought, and thought. The grasshopper hopped on to her shoulder and whispered into her ear, 'Never mind, Zara. It happens. You are still too young to appreciate the gesture. The monitor is the gatekeeper to the wisdom of this world. He sits by the river all day. He's been doing this for years. And then, he interprets the river's flow to Clus.'

'Clus?' What's that?' Zara raised a brow.

'Why? Creatures like us,' the grasshopper laughed. 'The frog who guided you here is a gatekeeper as well. And so is the elephant who blows his trumpet all day. But, above all these creatures and the rest of us, the river is the final gatekeeper, guiding wandering spirits like you and me to our final destination across its opposite bank, beyond the Ah!nandita Hills, atop the Moonshine Mount, where we all seek paradise.

'Aha!' Zara thought aloud. 'No wonder the river, too, flaunts the arrogance of the gatekeeper, whereas all she needs to do is keep flowing to eternity, beyond the cycle of the earth and the sky.'

'And that's exactly how each of us, at every level of awareness, discover that every creature here is a gatekeeper of wisdom. We all draw our arrogance from access control to the ultimate wisdom that really seems beyond our individual grasp,' the grasshopper went on.

'Oh! So, now that even I have acquired a drop of that wisdom, the same applies to me as well,' Zara jumped. 'I, too, am the gatekeeper, in my own sorta way.'

'Yes, dear Zara,' the grasshopper said. 'That's quite true. At every level, we all believe and allow ourselves into believing that "I am the gatekeeper, and you are the seeker to whom I shall pass on my wisdom, that you, in turn, shall impart to others." In the process, at every level, we want the next individual down the knowledge stairway to believe that "they are the gatekeeper, while I really am the Lord."'

'That's a nice game indeed,' Zara turned to the grasshopper.

'Come, you play gatekeeper, while I play the Lord.'

By now, the creatures had begun to disperse in ones and twos and in fives and tens. The grasshopper, too, hopped off Zara's shoulders and, soon, flew out of sight. Zara turned to the river from where she had parked herself, now on the second step from the water. The river took one wide glance at Zara and smiled.

And then, she resumed her graceful flow. In silence.

'Are you looking at me?' Zara asked the river.

Chapter 4

It had been quiet by the bank for sometime now. The sun had reached mid sky, its morning pleasantness giving way to midday scorn. Droplets of sweat had started gathering on Zara's forehead as she shaded her eyes with her palms, her feet dipped in water.

'Hi, Zara, still wondering?' the frog appeared from nowhere and parked himself next to her. 'Come, let's take a break under the peepul tree up there on the promenade and introduce you to the wonders of my world.'

And so, the frog hopped one step at a time, from one to two, from two to three, from three to four, from four to five, from five to six, from six to seven, from seven to eight, from eight to nine. Zara turned around and hopped. And hop, hop, hop, she climbed. And the moon waxed and waned with every hop. And with each step, Zara grew taller and taller. And so, she reached the promenade.

Squatting there was the monitor lizard.

'Access control,' remembered Zara.

Seeing Zara up there in the company of the frog, the lizard lost his cool, his knuckles knocking, knock, knock, knock; his shoulders straightened, head erect.

'Out ya go, you silly girl,' the lizard kicked the air. Frightened, Zara lost her balance and tumbled down the steps.

'This isn't the place for you,' she heard the lizard shout.

Humiliated and hurt, Zara collected herself and walked down to where she had come from, by the waterside, her head lowered, tears welling up her eyes, as the frog, disturbed and ashamed, hopped by her side.

By the time Zara had climbed down the steps, she somewhat regained her composure, as she sat down by the river, the frog by her side.

'Never mind, Zara. Denial denies you the sense of importance in life,' the river remarked, as she flowed on.

It wasn't long before the frog croaked at Zara once more.

'Come on Zara, let's give it another try.'

Puzzled, Zara looked right and left, and then, stood up, her face lit up once more. And hop, hop, hop, they climbed.

The monitor was still squatting on the promenade when they reached the top. This time, he signalled Zara to sit. And as Zara dusted the floor to sit face-to-face with the lizard, the frog hopped over to his side, facing Zara.

'What have you learnt little girl?' the lizard asked, as Zara raced her mind, thinking why she was so different from the rest of the creatures by the bank.

And how she had patiently waited by the water all these years, as the worms crawled to and fro in their mad scramble for survival. Then, picking up on how the lizard had admonished her in the morning, Zara asked him to guess her age.

'You must be, well, well, well, eight . . . or nine . . . or ten.' the monitor replied.

'Ha! I am much older than you think I am, dear Lizzy. I am certainly much older than most of the creatures gathered here. I am as old as Rivah! I flowed down here, from high up in the mountains, the day she came alive at the glacier's tongue. That's when I, too, was born in the dark. And now, I have been here by the bank for as long as I can remember.' For once, the lizard was nonplussed.

'It's not that I am ageing while I am young, it's just that I am young even though I have aged,' Zara laughed.

'O Lizzy! you have learnt to look at the glass half empty, but you still need to fill up your tumbler before your wisdom can flow like Rivah! Small wonder, your knowledge ends with age imprisoning you to a lifetime as gatekeeper.

'Maybe, dear Lizzy, you are content being the monitor that you are, but that cannot be the end. Because, after all, in the end, there is really no end. Life just goes on, and on, and on. So that we can merge our being in the other, irrespective of where we are and when,' Zara smiled at the lizard and raised her arms.

Going round in a whirl, she let out the magic words she had first learnt from the river.

'Jo tu hai, so main hoon,

jo main hoon, so tu hai!'

The lizard looked at Zara, amused, then smiled. 'You've got it all, Oh Zara! You've got it all. You have grasped the wisdom, climbing up these steps that I spent a lifetime to learn by this river's bank.'

'Just mind yourself and put that knowledge to good use, dear Zara. And if you have a doubt, just come by. I shall sharpen your thinking,' the lizard winked and darted off into the thicket behind the promenade.

Zara smiled and blew a kiss at Lizzy. She had understood the monitor just as well as the monitor had understood her.

It was late afternoon by the time Zara had climbed down to the waterfront. The sun was beginning to kiss the snow-clad peak of the tall, dark granite of the Moonshine Mount below which stood the pink sandstone Ah!nandita Hills, resplendent in the glow of the soon-to-be setting sun.

'That was well done, Zara, you handled your encounter with the lizard rather well. Learn to engage, disengage, and re-engage, dear girl,' the river said, flowing by.

Zara smiled.

'Well done, Zara,' the frog croaked aloud. Now, let's get up there, below the peepul tree, for you to meet my guests at tea.'

And so, they both ran up.

'Eeeks!' Zara screamed, 'You are not having them for snacks,' she shouted, staring disgustedly at the caterpillars gathered below the tree.

'Ha! Come easy, Zara,' the frog croaked. 'I come here to introduce my friends, who have come to the river from afar, not to eat them up.' And then, turning towards the creepy crawlies, the frog said, 'Zara, can you tell them why they live such a short life?'

'Hmmm!' Zara hesitated, then wondered before taking a deep breath of fresh air.

And she laughed, 'They live such a short life because Froggy eats them up all.'

'Hahaha!' the caterpillars laughed in one voice, even as the embarrassed frog blew his face in anger.

'Don't be stupid, Zara,' the frog admonished. I asked you the question in all seriousness.

'Come on, learn to take a joke, Froggy,' Zara reprimanded him.

And then, she said, 'What you get to see, dear, is only half the picture. You get to see life in slices. The caterpillars never really fail the life test. They actually grow out of that life, feeding on what they have till they can feed no more. And when they stop feeding, they stop growing any bigger. That's when they go into the hiding of their darkness within, seeking an answer to what's in store, even as the world around writes them off. Yet, deep within, in the wisdom of their souls, the caterpillars transcend their physical beings to emerge as beautiful butterflies. That's the wonder of their wisdom. They grow from prosperity to richness, from beauty to wonder. O Froggy! For the caterpillars, their bodies may ground to dust, but their souls live on till they acquire a newer form.'

The caterpillars nodded appreciatively.

'Well said, Zara,' said the river, rising up. 'Construct, deconstruct, and reconstruct to stay in touch and remain relevant. That's how you can all live happily ever after.'

Chapter 5

At sundown, Zara sat back, lazing . . . watching the ethereal display of light and sound by the river. The glow-worms danced in the dark to the chime of the thousand bells and blows of the thousand conch shells. The thousand lamps came floating downriver in a thousand leaf cups before ascending heavenwards in the distance. And the Moonshine Mount dazzled in the glare of the full moon matching the resplendence of the thousand gemstones atop the Peacock Ridge.

And the dance floors in the metros beyond the Peacock Ridge woke up to heady music as pretty damsels gyrated to shrill excited whistles from a hundred leering faceless bystanders.

'Your world is unreal, Zara, don't get trapped by your illusions,' said the river. 'Our mind lures us forever to the sights and sounds of its own apparitions. What you get to see of yourself in this world, dear Zara, whether in the reflection of the pool or the dazzle around you is only a miniaturised representation of the eternal whole. Just like you saw the enormous sun as a tiny ball in the pool when you first looked yourself up in my water on that hot summer day, everything you see around is a miniaturisation of this never-ending cosmos.'

Zara sat listening to the faint sweet voice of the river in the surrounding wilderness.

'Those glow-worms, Zara, and those gemstones, and the glow in the horizon from the city lights beyond the Peacock Ridge, you have enjoyed them all. Now, look up at the sky,' said the river.

Zara looked up at the stunning night sky, with billions and billions of stars twinkling, far brighter and more enchanting than all the light she had seen so far.

'Look Zara, look deep, and soak yourself completely in the joys of your imagination,' the river went on. 'Each of those stars you see in the distance is far, far bigger than any gemstone you will find around this world. In fact, each of those stars is several times bigger than the sun. Why, they are even a million times bigger than this world where you were born,' the river went on.

'It beats me how it could be so,' said Zara. 'There is nothing as big as my world. The sun is so big, and so powerful, and so strong. Even this earth, where I am, is so many times bigger than the sun and the moon and everything else in the sky. I can see them all, just as I can see the stars right now.'

'Just so, Zara,' said the river. 'But the earth actually goes around the sun and is what it is because of it. And the sun is actually among the smaller stars that make up this Universe of your creation. It's just that you get to see what you must from where you are stationed in life and at what time of the day or night. It is just as with the sun, that's really what it is, but you see it in its various moods of the day because of where you are positioned from it.'

'Is that so?' Zara asked. 'All this sounds too complicated for my age. Is this Universe really an illusion of my mind? Right now, I can dance with the glow-worms on the promenade, climb up the Peacock Ridge tomorrow, and pick up those gemstones one day. And some time, when I grow up, I can even lose myself in the dazzle of the city lights to the applause of a thousand hands. The stars?'

'You can even reach the stars,' the river said. 'Nothing is impossible, dear Zara, in this illusion of your creation. That is how your world goes around. Whatever you do, do it with firmness and resolve, and you shall reach your destination. The force of your intellect, alone, can help you achieve your end, little girl.'

'Aha!' Zara replied, pondering. 'I am still too young to reach someplace.'

'But nothing stops you from using the power of your knowledge, from reaching where you want to be, just like you used your power against a million other bubbles to reach where you are now.'

'How did I do it?' Zara asked, raising a brow.

'You did it because you knew it even deep inside the bubble that imagination held your world together. That's how you outsmarted the others in negotiating your destination. In reality, where you are and where you reach are as much true or false as your desire to be where you want to be. Nothing else matters.'

'Is that so? You mean it? Nothing else matters?' Zara asked.

'Yes, indeed. When you know that and believe it as such, you do not hurt others,' the river came back. 'When you know that you are actually the monster of your own power, you rest in humility and in love of all. But that's another story I'll tell you another day,' the river told Zara.

'But please, tell me more,' Zara fussed, kicking the air, 'I love to hear your voice.'

'Hehe!' the river laughed. 'I can see you getting charmed by my words. But beware, Zara, the charm and attraction of my thirst is a far greater illusion than the thirst for glamour that will draw you now. Beware! Involve yourself with a situation only as much as you are needed.'

'And how do I do that?' asked Zara.

'First, dear Zara, keep your mind in balance. Don't waver at whatever you see around. Statis of mind is essential.'

'Hmmm!' Zara nodded.

'Next, keep your senses under control. Never, ever get excited. When you do that, you rid yourself of your dilemma of differentiating between what's good and bad. What's real, what's virtual.'

'And why is that important?' Zara asked.

'Just look at me, Zara,' the river said, 'I don't discriminate between who I like and who I don't, between the rich and the poor. That's because I have nothing to prove, no matter how others perceive me. I have no war to win. I am here only to quench the thirst of whoever needs my water. I was alive before I was born, and I shall remain alive after I die, sometimes as water, at other times as cloud, snow or ice, and at still other times, as just hot air. Yet, at all times, I am what I am. Neither did I bring anything else along when I arrived on the earth as water, nor will I carry anything else away when I ride the sky as vapour.'

'So, in the end, it's all a zero-sum game,' Zara wondered aloud.

'I love games with a love-all ending.'

'Wow! That's a lesson well learnt,' the river told Zara. 'The fun is in loving one and all. I'll tell you more. For now, it's good night all. See you tomorrow!'

Chapter 6

An eerie silence descended by the bank that night as darkness engulfed the surroundings. Haunting shadows of the Peacock Ridge, the Moonshine Mount, and the Ah!nandita Hills loomed above the river. The glow in the distant eastern sky from the city lights was gone. There were no glow-worms dancing on the bank, no sound of bells and conch shells. The river, gurgling in the enveloping silence, had turned pitch dark, as if a lake of ink had spilt over in a giant flow in the distant mountains.

After everyone had gone to bed, the frog quietly hopped over to Zara and woke her up, 'Hey, Zara, wake up.'

Zara rubbed her eyes and shouted, 'Now what?' It had been a long day and she needed to sleep.

'Sssh!' the frog whispered. 'Zara, you've been with the river for a long time now. What's been your experience so far? The river asked me to find out.'

'When did she do that?' Zara shot back.

And then, turning to the river, she said, 'O Rivah! Froggy tells me you want to know my feelings. I have none. I shed my feelings high up in the mountains at the tongue of the glacier, the moment I came riding you here. I shed my emotions up there. I do not doubt what you say. But, as far as my feelings for you go . . . well, I do not seek any hope from you, nor do I despair from your presence. Every time you speak to me, I see my reflection in you, and it feels nice. And it feels good to feel nice.'

'It feels good to feel nice,' the frog repeated. 'It feels good to spread those feel-good words around.' And he hopped away into the surrounding darkness.

Zara lay down, turning on her side, facing the river, waiting to catch her sleep. It was to be a long wait. She lay there and thought. And thought and thought and thought, wondering if, indeed, she had renounced her feelings and emotions up there in the mountains at the glacier's tongue.

'Was I being true to my words or was I playing mind games?' she asked herself, self-doubt consuming her mind. Had she been arrogant, she would have behaved as such, Zara thought, not couched her attitude in sweet nothings.

And she told herself, 'Yes, on the face of it, I was being true.'

Zara had renounced her feelings and emotions before embarking on the long river ride. That's how she had come to be here, alone and all by herself, unlike all the other creatures that had come to the riverbank in twos and threes and fours . . .

'Yet, there must be a lingering feeling of attachment, tucked somewhere deep in my heart,' Zara told herself. 'I cannot be so heartless.'

And Zara's mind raced from situation to situation,

from creature to creature—the elephant, the monitor lizard, the frog, the grasshopper, the dragonfly, the butterfly, the bee—scanning her deepest feelings of love and hatred. And with every imagined situation and creature she kept reassuring herself, 'Yes, it's true. I left my emotions behind.'

And then, her mind raced backwards, up the river's course, past the narrow gullies and steep gorges, climbing the fall in backward motion. Back, back, back, past rapids and bends, at double the speed at which she had descended, in flashback motion till she came to rest at the mouth of the glacier encased in the plasma bubble in which she had once arrived at the riverbank.

And there, the glacier's tongue licked the bubble as Zara lay crumpled on her side, the size of an atom, looking right into the bubble that rested next to her, encasing her lookalike.

'Whooaaa! That's Zara again, in my likeness,' Zara told herself.

'Now, what if I reach out to her?' she wondered. 'I only need to reach my finger out to get a feel of her by my side.' And so, raising her right arm, Zara extended her index finger from inside the bubble. And her likeness raised her left arm mirroring Zara's movement, extending her index finger toward Zara.

She had almost touched the inner wall of her own bubble when, suddenly, she stopped.

'What if my bubble bursts? Will the other bubble burst as well? And what if it does and that other Zara of my likeness falls down smeared in a splash of red? Oh God! She's such a tiny creature. How can I ever hurt her?'

And so, Zara asked herself, 'What if Zara, my lookalike, disappears at my sudden touch now that I am so close to bursting her bubble? Would I then feel her loss? Would I mourn her?'

Zara tried to avoid the fountain of questions spouting forth from her mind.

'Oh! She's such an innocent. She deserves all my emotions,' she consoled herself, staring at her lookalike. And at once, she felt scared as the mop of hair on her head stood on its end and fear slowly crawled up her shivering spine.

After a long, long time, Zara's mind had been overpowered by the fear of loss. She was no longer having fun. She was no longer feeling nice as she had boasted only a little while ago to the river. Her deepest feelings were out in the open.

'So, have I been true to Rivah!?' Zara asked herself. 'Indeed, have I been true to myself?' she wondered.

CHAPTER 7

Zara looked around and, then, looked up at the sky.

'Wassup?' she asked.

Not a soul stirred that new moon night. It hadn't been a pleasant day for her. In fact, it had been quite nasty. Never since she had come to be perched on the wedge had her emotions hung in such precarious balance, trapped in the illusion of her mind, racing back and forth along the course of the river between the glacier's tongue and the Ah!nandita Hills; the ghastly image of her lookalike smeared in red, falling off a bursting bubble high up in the freezing mountain tormented her.

And Zara kept wondering. And she kept asking herself if she had made a false boast to the river about renouncing her fears and emotions at birth. And yet, she reassured herself that she hadn't lied. It was the fear of the unknown within that had surfaced in her mind because of her deep introspection of the night before.

And Zara kept reminding herself, 'Yes, what I had told the river was true. I hadn't lied.' After all, it was true that she had met her lookalike high up in the mountain at the mouth of the glacier, moments before she slipped out in the warmth unleashed by the glacier's tongue in the maddening race to her present destination, rupturing each colliding bubble in her struggle for survival. And Zara had deliberately shed her emotions during that long and eventful life-defining journey, distancing herself from her feelings and attachments.

So now, there was no point recollecting past images of her millions of lookalikes encased in millions upon millions of plasma bubbles.

'Give up, give up, give up! Give up on the images of your mind and tell yourself there is no other face on the face of this earth that looks quite like yours. There's no point thinking about what no longer is,' she told herself.

And she reasoned, 'So, what if my lookalike is gone. That indeed was her destiny, just as I will meet my destiny one day.

My lookalike only lives in me.'

That's how Zara tried to overcome her fear. Yet, the more she thought of it, the more she fell in love with her image, and the more she panicked, remembering a million innocent faces, lying calm, encased in a million plasma bubbles.

Zara wished to run back to where she had come from.

Catching her in a pensive mood, the river whispered, 'Why are you so sad, dear Zara? Why do you feel so lonesome tonight?

If your mind makes you anxious, resolve all your issues right now. After all, it's part of the game. Hope and fear are the opposite banks through which I flow alone.'

'I see,' Zara said in a hushed voice.

'The obsession with me consumes my mind, dear Zara,' the river said, breaking the numbing silence. 'The me and mine of those who have cause pain to those who do not. When I rest in my arrogance, I miss the boat to my destination in the sky, shrinking with time into a cesspool instead.'

'On this dark foreboding night, O little girl!' the river went on, 'ask yourself on which of the three shall you ride the sky: knowledge, imagination, or action?'

Zara looked up. She hadn't a clue.

'The answer, Zara, is simple,' the river said. 'Riding the arrogance of any one of three will not help you reach the sky. You need knowledge, imagination, and action in their unadulterated forms to merge with the canvas above; just as I do, little Zara, from ice to water to vapour.'

'The river helps you know yourself. Kill the I in you every day, kill all that you feel is yours.'

'You are doing well, Zara,' the frog hopped over to her side from the middle of nowhere. 'You know what, Zara, each of these nine steps that you see by the riverbank are the nine steps of learning the great lesson of life. Come with me, let me guide you there.'

And so, that moonless night, Zara hopped up to the promenade in step with the frog. And when they had reached the top, both turned towards the river.

'Here, as we stand on the first step of life, we listen to the voice of wisdom,' the frog said.

'We listen to the voice of wisdom,' repeated Zara, hopping after the frog to the step below.

And so, a year passed by . . .

'And here, as we stand on the second step of life, we read the flow of the river of life.'

'And we read the flow of the river of life,' repeated Zara, hopping down another step.

And another year was gone . . .

'And here, as we stand on the third step of life, we kill all our previous assumptions.'

'And we kill all our previous assumptions,' said Zara.

And so, with every step, a year passed.

'And here on the fourth step of life, we imbibe the new lessons of life.'

'And we imbibe the new lessons of life,' said Zara.

'And here on the next step of life, we spread the good word around.'

'And we spread the good word around,' said Zara.

'And here on the next step of life, we rejoice in song and dance.'

'And we rejoice in song and dance,' said Zara, her arms raised, doing her now favourite whirl.

'And here on the seventh step of life, we commune with our own reflections,' said the frog.

'And here, we commune with our reflections,' said Zara.

'Having done so, here on the eighth step of life, we

play with one and all, in the spirit of sharing and love.'

'And we love one and all,' said Zara.

'And then, on the ninth and final step of life . . .' said the frog, pausing a while.

'And on the ninth step?' repeated Zara, narrowing her eyes, waiting to catch the lesson.

'It's total surrender. We immerse ourselves in the river of life, content, and coming to terms with who we really are.'

'We come to terms with who we really are,' said Zara, raising her arms above her head, jumping with joy at the end of nine years.

"Thank you, Froggy. Thanks, thanks, thanks! That was indeed a wonderful lesson, I really feel nice about who I am. It really feels so good.'

'Thank you, Froggy! Thank you, Rivah!'

Zara was beside herself with joy, her dreadful night seemed finally over.

Then, looking up to the heaven above, she wondered, 'Where did that thought come from? For whom did it come? Why did it come? Why was I so scared?'

And saying so, Zara told herself, 'Yes, I am in love with my lookalike, because my inner voice tells me to be in love with my innocence. The rest of the plot doesn't matter. What matters is that I arouse my emotions within for that which is pure. And yet, remain detached from the scenery around and the urge to hold on.'

Unnoticed by Zara, the first rays of the sun had

begun to wink from behind the Peacock Ridge some distance away from where Zara had been standing all night on the riverbank. And in the soft glow of dawn, a giant bubble rose from the water.

It had been twenty-one years since Zara had arrived at the bank. Standing tall, she faced her infant lookalike crouched inside the bubble, staring at Zara, a large smile pasted on her face.

'Connect, disconnect, reconnect, Zara,' her lookalike said. 'It's fun!'

And bang! The bubble burst. Zara rubbed her eyes. Her lookalike had finally disappeared, never to haunt her again. There was no one around. Only Zara and the river flowing by.

Chapter 8

Zara dipped her feet in the ice-cold water of the river, one at a time. Then, she pulled them out. It was late autumn and the mountains higher up had started freezing. There was no one at the bank yet. And though she had spent the whole night awake, she was remarkably fresh. Zara dipped her feet and pulled them back again and again till she was certain that she could endure the chill.

And, as the first bells started chiming in the distance, she slipped in, waist-deep in water. Zara never felt the need for ritual ablutions in the river as it had been with the other creatures, day after day. It was just that the river was there, and Zara felt refreshed.

From where she stood in water, Zara caught the flight of the tittiris on the opposite bank, heading north across the river face of the Ah!nandita Hills, just as she had seen them when she was perched atop the wedge in a bubble.

Zara laughed, turned eastwards, towards the rising sun, and laughed louder. She turned to the river and laughed . . . still louder. And the wind picked up her mirth and blew off in the path of the birds. And the bells rang louder, heading south from upriver, drowning Zara's laughter.

And Zara raised her hands, running them through her long auburn hair, and slipped into the water chanting, 'Give up, give up, give up!' This was Zara's first plunge into the river. And now that she was deep in the water, gliding among the fish, Zara came face-to-face with the giant mahseer.

All these years, she had seen the mahseer from above the water, submerged still among several other big and small creatures of its like—calm and composed.

'How do you do, Mah!seer?' Zara asked.

'I am fine, thank you, Zara. Welcome to the river! How do you do?'

'Good,' replied Zara.

'Come, lemme show you around my parlour. It's remarkably quiet today,' said the big fish and both glided into midstream with the current, Zara rising once in a while to the surface to catch her breath.

'Tell me, Mah!seer,' asked Zara, 'how do you breathe under water? I have to climb up to the surface so often.'

'That's not at all difficult, dear,' the mahseer said. 'Remember what the river told you the other day? It's not enough to have only knowledge. Nor is it enough to build on imagination alone. And it sure isn't enough to work hard. You need knowledge, imagination, and hard work in their unadulterated forms to come together to merge with the sky.'

'Oh yes, I do, but all that's about the sky, dear Mah!seer, that's made of air, not water.'

'Ha!' laughed the mahseer, 'It's pretty much the

same with water. Water, after all, is made of nothing but air, one-part oxygen that you breathe in, and two-parts hydrogen. And I suck that oxygen out of water by putting my knowledge, imagination, and hard work to use.'

'How wonderful!' said Zara. 'You have arrived indeed, Mah!'

'And so have you, dear Zara. Remember those magic words, "Jo tu hai, so main hoon."'

'Jo main hoon, so tu hai,' smiled Zara, climbing to the surface to catch her breath again when a wild fig dropped into the water with a loud *phukt* sound. Zara looked up. The giant bee was hovering overhead, trying to listen to the conversation.

'Tell me, O gatekeeper!' the bee buzzed at the mahseer. 'Who does the river really love?'

'Aha!' the mahseer came back. 'That's such a tricky question. The river loves all those who gather by its banks.'

'Na, na, na,' protested Zara. 'The river loves all, equally.'

'How do you say that?' argued the mahseer. 'How can the river love the cunning, the devious, and the fraud?'

'Ha! There's the cunning, the devious, and the fraud in each of us, dear Mah!seer. It depends on where we are, when, and why.'

Zara had finally joined the great existential debate among the creatures on the river's bank, beyond the concerns of her own immediate desires.

'Enough of hot air,' the river joined in. 'Now, listen carefully to what I say.'

'When both our mind and intellect are strong, which one do we shun?' she seemed to be obviously referring to Zara.

'I am arrogant that I know all. I am the Lord of all I survey.'

Never mind if you feel so, it's quite natural,' the river said. 'While it's true that the body harbours emotions and sensations, it is the wise alone who know how to bring them under control and use them to right effect. By taking the opposite route to where our emotions and sensations lead us, we can convert them into our most potent weapons and use them to serve our purpose in life,' the river went on.

'How does one do that, Rivah!?' the bee joined in.

'Be-ezee! You do that by first controlling your desire. But desire the good of all. Then share your joy and pleasure with everybody around. To do good to yourself, dear Be-ezee!, first do good to others,' the mahseer interrupted.

'I have already made that my creed,' said the bee.

'How's that so, you stinging bee?' Zara mocked aloud.

'You little witch,' the bee swooped down ready to sting, taking offence at Zara's stinging criticism. That's when the mahseer jumped out of the water and pulled Zara down under.

'Have patience, Zara. You'll know more with time. Right now, just listen to the river, young lady,' the mahseer said.

'I am so sorry,' Zara said.

'Never mind. So, where was I?' the river went on. 'Ah yes! Make yourself like me for the others to quench their thirst. The river never remembers who came in or who went out. It doesn't even wait for anybody as it flows on. The river feels the presence of visitors but doesn't drown in their joy or sorrow. It ought to be the same with your mind that harbours both the good and the evil.'

'And how can it be the same with the mind?' the bee asked.

'What use we make of our mind depends entirely on us,' said the river.

'Absence of desire leads to equanimity of attitude towards both the good and the evil, towards what is yours and what belongs to others. The cunning, the devious, the fraud, all belong to my Universe, just like you and the rest, Mah!seer. And I treat everyone alike, keeping my emotions in check. That's what I call true love.'

'I understand you well,' the bee came around, 'but how do I react when the world stings me, just as when young Zara called me a stinging creature not so long ago?'

'That's the dilemma of your identity. You can't really do a thing about that, dear Be-ezee! Criticism is bound to be your shadow as long as you choose to be what you want to be,' said the river.

'Get it?' the frog appeared from nowhere. 'I got

that a long time ago,' he said.

'And what did you get, dear Froggy?' Zara asked.

'I got it a long time ago to keep my emotions in check to maintain my mental poise.'

'Treat all your five emotions of lust, anger, desire, longing, and arrogance as your retainers in order to control your mind,' said the river. 'In all of creation it is the mind alone that does not perform to command.'

'So, what do I do?' Zara asked.

'Live in the fear of your own self within. Live in fear of auto-deactivation. That's how you will also deactivate your mind. Only then will you be able to use your emotions as weapons under your exclusive command.'

The river laughed!

CHAPTER 9

Zara had spent the whole day swimming and was now beginning to tire.

'It's been a long swim for you,' the mahseer remarked.

'Yes, and I am beginning to feel the strain. My muscles are pulling,' Zara said.

'Hehe!' the river laughed. 'When you swim, you mustn't talk; when you talk, you mustn't swim, Zara. That's the first lesson about negotiating a river. The next, of course, is to keep it simple and straight. If you are here for fun, just splash around in my water. Nothing comes from getting too smart.'

'Why do you say that?' Zara protested.

'It's not for you alone, Zara,' the river said. 'I speak to all. By now, you would have met several creatures by my bank. If you observe them carefully, Zara, first, there are those who come here to bathe and move on. And then, there are others who rinse their mouths and spit out the water. Those who are really smart, drink my water and leave nothing to waste. Those who use my water just for a wash or a quick rinse by my bank hardly take anything away, feeling nice and clean for the moment, and polluting my water instead. It's only the wise, like that giant banyan by my western bank, who actually soaks my water and give comfort to one and all.'

That night as darkness fell and Zara prepared to sleep, the frog silently hopped on to her lap.

'How's it going so far, Zara?' he asked.

'It's been good. I like Rivah!'

Then, looking conspiratorially at her, the frog said in a hushed voice, 'You know what, Zara? In the end, there's nothing in the river. No fish, no worm, no creature. There's even no water, no air. There's nothing at all. It's just a big hoax for the river to keep going on and on.'

'Just watch her flow from earth to sky. And it's the same with all of us. Our desperate need to survive in this harsh world makes us go around in circles, building one dream after chasing another, to stay in constant joy. That, and that alone, is real.'

Zara was dumbstruck.

Chapter 10

It was late afternoon in peak summer. The mercury was soaring. The river had completely disappeared by now, taking with it the fishes and weeds, exposing massive boulders, rocks and pebbles on the dry river bed, its banks devoid of their lush green cover; the plants withered from the searing heat. The creatures, too, were all gone—the ants, the houseflies, the bees, the butterflies, the dragonflies, the grasshoppers, and the frog. The only souls left by the bank were the monitor lizard and Zara. Both met up every now and then under the peepul tree. The lizard now flaunted a slate grey colour that camouflaged well with the stones on the river bed; fair Zara, now dishevelled, had acquired an uneven tan.

The peepul tree still sported signs of life, providing shade for the weary traveller by the riverside. The bees, too, had been hanging around, their massive hive on the peepul's branch dripping with honey.

Once in a while, a cool breeze swept by the banks at dusk or dawn, but there was no sign of water raining down from the sky or rushing down in a torrent from the mountaintop.

The bells had long stopped ringing. And so had the conch shells. No more lamps in leaf cups floated down to where Zara sat, by the bank.

The glow-worms, too, were mostly gone, but for an occasional visitor at dusk.

The gemstones atop the Peacock Ridge still glistened by night, but the dazzle atop the Moonshine Mount was gone. Somehow, in the barren emptiness of their surroundings, they seemed to be robbed of glamour. The action or whatever there was to it, seemed to have shifted to the metro, far, far away beyond the ridge, where the dazzle of the night gave way to the despair of morn with clockwork precision. And creatures gathered under the glittering city lights, in dark and foreboding alleys, under drainpipes and in the gutters, under beds and washbasins, routinely fumigated out of their dens and trampled under a thousand feet in their grim battle for survival.

Thus, day made way for night and night made way for morn, with little sign of hope, when, suddenly, one morning the bees sent out a buzz, abandoning their hive, and rushing towards the bank.

'She's coming, she's coming, O Rivah!' they cried. 'Word's reached us from the top that the river is on its way to the bank.'

Zara, napping under the peepul tree, woke up to the excitement stirred by the bees. She looked around to find the swarm rushing to the bank as their buzz grew louder and louder.

And as the drone came nearer, the sky turned dark, just as it had several summers ago when she first sat by the river after falling off her bubble and hopping to the shore. And she heard the familiar croak as she rushed across the promenade to the steps below, taking one step at a time.

'Come down fast, Zara,' the frog croaked aloud. 'The river is on its way.'

'Sure, I'm on my way, too, Froggy,' she laughed.

Down there on the steps, Zara found herself an absolutely wonderful spot to sit, anticipating the depth of the river's flow past the bank. There, she worked herself to a perfect posture as questions raced through her mind.

'What should I ask Rivah!?' Zara wondered.

And as she reflected, she told herself, 'Actually, I have come to the bank with absolutely nothing to talk about. It's been a long summer and I do not even have the headspace to learn something new. I first need to absorb all that Rivah! taught me all these years and carry on with life. I should have possibly stayed back under the peepul tree to contemplate on what I should do next.'

And Zara sat there and thought and thought and thought. And she told herself not to worry. After all, she had climbed down the steps to satiate the lust of her eyes, to watch the river up close after a long dry spell. And as she sat there thinking hard, she began to unclutter her mind.

The creatures, too, had begun to pack the steps by now, closing in on Zara, as one jabbed her legs into her side and another crammed her from the other end, making her uncomfortable.

And as she sat in her perfect upright posture, shoulders erect, just like the lizard, Zara closed her eyes, raised her head skywards, breathed deeply, and chanted, 'Give up, give up, give up!'

And thus, she went on, when midway, she was overcome by pain, brought about by the constant irksome pushing and shoving from the crawlies crowding about her. Yet, Zara resolved to carry on, sitting erect, her eyes shut tight.

And while she carried on with her stubborn resolve to continue sitting upright, her focus began to waver before the vacant altar of the long-lost river.

And so, sooner than she had presumed, Zara almost pleaded with herself to be relieved of her self-inflicted pain.

'There's no point sitting in meditation. It leads nowhere,' came a voice from above. The dragonfly was hovering overhead. Zara finally abandoned her thoughts. Her pain growing rapidly, she was overwhelmed by the urge to quit without getting to meet the river. If anything restrained her from quitting, it was the thought of standing up and walking out in front of so many other creatures and the very real possibility of trampling several of them under her feet.

'What if I hurt them? That would be catastrophic. Would I also expose my arrogance? Would I be subject of scorn?' The questions ran helter-skelter through her mind.

Whatever engaging conversation she might have

had set herself for the river, now seemed distant in the chaos by the bank.

So, Zara consoled herself. 'Pain leads to gain,' she reasoned, 'I need to get back my focus.'

And even as she spoke to herself, inventing one excuse after another only to hang around, the grasshopper broke the silence in the anti-climax of the moment.

'It will still be a while before the river arrives by the bank.

There's no point hanging on.'

'Oh no!' Zara sighed, looking around. There was no sign of anguish on a single face. Instead, the creatures seemed to let off a collective sigh of relief. All this while, millions of them had shared Zara's agony, waiting anxiously for the river. Zara climbed up to the promenade, marvelling at the river's evasive power, anticipating the mass discomfort of so many creatures in her wait.

'Was that telepathy or a mere coincidence?' Zara wondered, taken in by the river's unanticipated absence.

Back on the promenade, the frog introduced her to one of the builder ants. Excited, Zara asked the ant to interpret her feelings.

'O Zara! What I have learnt from the river in all these years is that there is really nothing to learn. What you still get to learn is: "I am what I am."'

'We are prone to fret and fume about our unfulfilled desires, like anticipating the flow of the river. Yet, all that we see around, dear Zara, all this creation, is the creation of energy that actually resides in you and me and manifests as our imagination first. This Universe, Zara, is the creation of our several desires. It is the product of our energy in motion. And when our imagination flounders, we feel sapped of energy.'

'What's energy?' Zara asked.

'Energy is that that makes us go. It's either dormant or in motion. Nobody can see that energy. We can only feel it.'

'I can understand energy in motion, it happens with me all the time as I sit by the river and imagine. And then, move to make things happen. But how do I recognise energy when it's asleep?' Zara asked.

'Well, if you recognise one, you can recognise the other. When it sleeps, the river stops its flow,' the ant replied.

'When no desire, no movement in this world of yours arouses your passion, your energy, then, is dormant. There is no distress. There is no pain. And that state of emptiness, when there is no passion, no pain, no joy, is the state of bliss,' the ant went on.

'Bliss, Zara, is a state of no feeling.'

'But I always get excited,' said Zara.

'I understand,' said the ant. 'It is one thing to get excited, but it's quite another to arouse yourself to a state of euphoria. That happens when your movement comes devoid of physical sensation.'

'I have felt such a state once in a while,' Zara told

the ant. 'When my world moves by vigorously by the bank. And I just sit and watch.'

'That's right, it happens when your imagination works to such a stage, when you just let it be. It's exactly the moment before a ripe fruit falls to the ground. That state is also called Ah!nandita,' said the ant.

'Do you mean those pink sandstone hills across the river?' Zara asked.

'Yes, Zara, have you felt the emptiness of the other bank of the river, while all the action takes place on this? That's the state to be.'

'Tell me how it works,' Zara demanded.

'I'm not quite sure of that. It's just . . . there,' said the ant. 'Some things just happen.'

'I don't believe that. You must be knowing,' retorted Zara.

'Do you feel the blood flow in your veins? Do you know what pumps your heart? Nobody does. They happen. Every single day, every single moment of our lives wonderful things happen to us for which we have no explanation. All I know is that it happens because the energy that is within us is at work.'

'So life just goes on,' said Zara.

'Yes, on and on and on, till it's time to call it quits,' said the ant. 'That's time for energy to get some sleep. And we rest in bliss.

Energy, little girl, follows nobody's command.'

'So what?' Zara shot back, looking visibly irritated.

'Yeah, you are right. Except that I will teach you

a little trick. You can watch the river flow and learn from its motions to manipulate the flow of your energy at all times. The creature that retains control over its energy and, therefore, its emotions, eventually controls its Universe, Zara. That's what wisdom is all about.'

'That's fascinating. I will rule my own Universe one day,' said Zara.

'Yes, you will,' said the ant. 'Different creatures do different things to master their Universe. In the end, we need self-control to be happy at all times, not sad.'

'I get it, dear Anty,' smiled Zara. 'You know what? All these years that I have been by the river, one thing's repeatedly come to my mind—at any given point, we all keep standing on different landings on the staircase of life. Nobody quite knows where the staircase will eventually lead us to. But that doesn't really matter; what does is the flexibility of the mind to be able to negotiate its different landings.'

'Well said, Zara,' the ant replied. 'You have really arrived in life the day you accept everything coming your way with the same detachment, devoid of praise or remorse.'

'I got it,' yelled Zara.

'Then you got bliss as well,' said the ant. 'Bliss is when you remember nothing. It's when your creation becomes a series of moving images that don't stop in time.'

'Living in the moment, you mean?' Zara asked.

'Living in the moment, indeed,' said the ant.

It was to be a while before Zara would absorb the full import of her conversation with the ant. As they turned back from the bank, Zara wondered if she had seen the last of the river. And her excitement grew with time.

Gradually, Zara was overcome by anxiety.

The anxiety of what might be.

What if Rivah! didn't turn up again?

Chapter 11

That evening, Zara waited by the bank. The creatures, too, had come down at sundown. After a long, long break, the bells had started chiming in the distance. And slowly, the blow of conch shells filled the air. The glow-worms came in next, in ones and twos, and then, by the dozens. It had been a long and fruitless wait all day. But the creatures did not seem to give up on hope. The long, hot, and parched summer had made them anxious. Zara was no longer sure if the river would reappear.

She had spent long successive summers by the riverbank now. But it hadn't been so desperately hot before.

Earlier, there had always been a stream, or a pool, or even a puddle, just as it had been the first year she had arrived. This year had been the worst. Not a drop to be seen around.

And in all these years gone by, countless creatures had been enthralled by the river's sheer depth.

Zara had been a silent witness to the creatures' cravings by the eastern bank. She had been a witness to pleading creatures, ecstatic creatures, and awestruck creatures rejoicing in the river's abundance, though the river never seemed to get swayed by any single one of them.

And as Zara sat there pondering, her mind was once more overcome by anticipation of what may come about. Just like that.

Just about that time, Zara immersed herself in deep imagination of what might come about, she suddenly caught the lamps in leaf cups floating her way down the river. And on that crowded night she saw the river quietly reappear under the glare of the full moon night, in the dazzle of the Moonshine Mount and the glitter of the Peacock Ridge.

'Welcome Rivah! Hurrah!' the creatures rent the air, cheering at the sight of flowing water.

'Welcome Rivah!' Zara jumped up, excited.

And the river silently crept up to the bank in a rapid swell, in an unimaginable expanse, her depth unfathomable. Rising, rising, rising!

Zara was awestruck.

'Awesome!' she exclaimed as the river expanded in her mind.

And the river rushed in as the creatures rose one by one, and in dozens, and hundreds, and thousands in standing ovation, chanting: '*Hu va, hu va, hu va!*' meaning, splendid, splendid, splendid.

And as she filled up her banks, the river broke her silence:

> There's nothing to fear when you are in love. There's nothing to fear when you are not in hate. There's nothing to fear when you have nothing to prove.

And then, the river asked, 'What is it that keeps you unaware? The knower knows, they are aware within, never mind what your mind tells you. Just silence your turmoil within.'

Zara was taken aback, even as more and more questions came calling, 'If all one needs to do is look within, then why did all these creatures rush to the bank, as if in a mad scramble for survival?' she asked herself.

And in that silence, her mind opened up . . .

'Most of these creatures are running away from themselves. It makes no difference whether they are here or not. Yet, most are here in search of peace, in search of tranquillity, and, therefore, in search of liberation from the bondage of their own buzz. Sadly, neither do they find permanent peace nor permanent liberation. And so, they keep coming again, and again, and again, in their elusive search to quench their thirst.'

'You are right, Zara,' the river paused a while where she sat.

'Naked across my threshold all must pass.'

And then, turning to the creatures, she said, 'Most of you listen to your inner voice through one ear and take it out through the other, living this wise moment that comes from silent contemplation on my banks for as long as it lasts. It's time you realised that what you contemplate upon now, dear creatures of this world, contemplate upon the same when you are gone from here, should you seek abiding joy. For when you listen to your voice, you are fulfilled.'

'And what if you do?' croaked the frog, adding, 'Since the best way to disarm your opponent is not to make an appearance at all, it's probably best to shut out the noise of your mind.'

'So, who blinks first?' Zara asked.

'It's your arrogance, not fear that makes you disappear,' said the river.

'So, who blinks first?' Zara asked again.

'You may switch off for a while when in mental or physical distress,' the river went on, 'or when in self-doubt. That's when you look deep within. Spend more time with yourself to still your mind.'

The river seemed to have read Zara's mind on the go, anticipated her fears, and relieved her distress in the simplest words. Zara was amazed at her limitless depth.

'Appear, disappear, reappear, just like me,' the butterfly laughed.

'But, unlike the caterpillar, don't shut yourself from the outside world to transform from within,' the river came back. 'One day, you will know why. Don't shut your mind and get into a trance. Rather, surmount every boulder that comes your way,' the river said.

'Reconcile your thoughts each day, dear Zara, to overcome the dilemmas of your mind,' the frog butted in. 'Make use of your knowledge and wisdom to carry on through life.'

'Reflect, reflect, reflect within, as much as you reflect on me,' said the river. 'Work is wisdom, wisdom is work. Go, get working.'

And then, she burst forth signing:

> Put your mind on even keel O boatman!
> It's time to figure out
> Where your boat rests today
> Before you venture onwards.
> Put your mind on even keel O boatman!
> It's time to figure out
> Your real destination
> Before you row on.

Long, long ago, Zara had heard the river sing. The creatures joined in:

> . . . figure out
> Your real destination, O boatman!
> Before you row on.

That night, when the creatures were gone, Zara sat back, reflecting on the day gone by. Then, raising her face to the moonlit sky, she whispered:

> You are my fear, and you are my joy. I am taken by your arrogance, your dignity, your compassion. O Rivah! Please guide me through the course of my life.

Zara had given herself to the river completely. No questions asked.

Unknown to her, the frog had heard Zara. At once, he hopped on her lap, goading her to talk her heart out to the river.

Zara thought . . . and thought . . . and thought.

Chapter 12

It was midnight. The full moon gleamed overhead. There was a pleasant calm by the bank. Zara stood up, and said:

Dear Rivah!,

I came to your bank many moons ago, riding your wave in my arrogance, in the bubble of my imagination. I was an infant then. And one day, my bubble burst, exposing me to the rigours of life. Today, I am in my fullness, just as it is with the moon and just as it is with you after such a long, dry spell.

I have enjoyed every moment here by your bank, learning all I could about the meaning of life from you, but I need to learn lots more. Froggy gave me company during these eventful years, interpreting the various nuances of your flow.

He has been a friend, philosopher, and guide.

I have told this to Froggy, and I'll tell you this: my arrogance came from the absence of fear in my mind and my eagerness to probe. It also came from my ability to renounce.

Give up, give up, give up!

My arrogance never came from my inheritance,

which, I had none. I am sure you are aware of this. Every time I sat by your bank, I learnt something new. And yet, there was nothing new in whatever you said. There can be no greater learning than this. You taught me to fear the vastness of your expanse, which is also the vastness of my imagination. You taught me to fear the infinity of self. And then, you taught me to overcome my fear by submerging myself in my reflection in you.

That's another next great lesson of life.

Today, you have become both my fear and hope. It's so much in your nature, O Rivah!

In teaching me, you have also revealed to me that arrogance comes with dignity and humility.

Froggy has been pushing me hard to accept you as my master and benefactor and plunge into the depths of your wisdom. I wasn't convinced. But today, in all my arrogance, I accept you as the gatekeeper to the ultimate wisdom out of my own accord and free will. I do so not to please Froggy, but because I have learnt whatever you had to teach. All I need to do now is practise what you preach.

And, in all my humility, I accept you as my teacher. Dignity demands that I take one last plunge in your water before I call it a day by your bank and move on. But I'll wait for you to grant me that dignity.

As for Froggy, I'll always be grateful to him for being my first gatekeeper and mentor, who showed me the way to your bank when I was a toddler in real danger of getting drowned in the sudden gush of your water. He has been a wonderful gatekeeper to your wisdom.

Now, it is time for me to join my world and the routine of daily life in the great metro beyond the Peacock Ridge, under the neon lights for my chance encounter with the flashbulbs.

So long!

And Zara broke into a song:

> Come, lemme hold your hand
> And lead you to a distant land
> Where there's no sorrow, no tear,
> But lots of love around . . .

Zara waited. The river was silent. It flowed on.

Zara sat by the bank for the next couple of days and nights, hoping to hear the river invite her for a swim.

She had told the river: 'Dignity demands that I take one last plunge in your water before I call it a day. But I'll wait for you to grant me that dignity.' And so, Zara waited. Thinking! Expecting! Those words ringing in her ears. Yet, her opportunity never came.

'Do not demand dignity, dear Zara. Deserve dignity,' the frog croaked on her last night by the bank.

Chapter 13

It was daybreak on the promenade. Zara looked to the Peacock Ridge to face the rising sun. Then, she closed her eyes. It would be a while before she moved on towards the distant city. She was at the far end of the promenade away from the river, even as the rest of the creatures of her mind made their way to the waterfront. The bells chimed in the far distance to the accompaniment of the blow of conch shells. Soon, the steps were packed with the creatures, but Zara.

The river flowed as usual.

There was a nip in the air that carried the scent of intoxicating wild flowers.

Zara, her face to the sun, kept thinking. Thinking deep!

Presently, her eyes rested midstream on the still surface of the river, when, for a moment, she was taken aback by a blue lotus bud rising above the water.

'Wow! I never saw that before!' Zara exclaimed, peering into the midstream for a clearer view. And she rubbed her eyes, wondering if it were for real. And as Zara watched, the lotus unfolded its petals, one by one, a thousand times. And with it, Zara's mind peeled open, layer after layer of thought, her imagination in full bloom.

'The lotus has blossomed!' Zara told herself, her eyes sparkling, an enigmatic smile spreading across her face.

'I got it, I got it, I got it all,' Zara cried out, tears of joy rolling down her cheeks.

'I have discovered the cycle of life!'

'Hope gives way to fear, fear to hope!' she chanted.

'Joy gives way to sorrow, sorrow to joy.

Appear, disappear, reappear just as you connect, disconnect, reconnect.

Engage, disengage, re-engage just as you construct, deconstruct, reconstruct.

Begin. End. Begin all over again.

It's the one-nine-one circle of life.

Round and round and round.

It's all the same.

The I in you, the you in I.

We all go around in circles.

It's virtual. It's real.'

And then, Zara cried out for Froggy.

Down on the steps below, the creatures heard Zara break the morning silence. The frog, surprised, turned around at the voice of Zara calling out for him. Stamping on the crawlies all around, he jumped up the steps. And hop, hop, hop, he went.

Panting, he reached Zara and jumped high to land on her shoulder.

'There's two in one, just as there is one in two,' said Zara.

'Jo tu hai, so main hoon; jo main hoon, so tu hai,' she chanted.

The frog prodded Zara to run down to the river. 'Come, it's time you made a splash.'

The elephant, silently watching Zara's antics on the promenade all along, blew his trumpet loud and clear.

But by now, Zara was ready to leave.

'Please give me a lift, dear Elly,' she shouted. 'I have a life . . .'

And then, turning to the frog, she said, 'Just gimme a break!'

In the distance, at the bend right below the Peacock Ridge, Zara prodded the elephant to halt for a last glimpse of the river where she had spent so many years, soaking the wisdom of life. The elephant paused, then turned around in his languid pace—swaying gently from side to side—to face the river, its turquoise water shimmering in the morning sun.

Zara shaded her eyes with her palm and looked into the distance from the rise where she sat atop the elephant. The green-blue water snaked across a vast plain, kissing the mountains goodbye at the feet of the Ah!nandita Hills, now dwarfed in view from where Zara was stationed.

The black solid granite of the Moonshine Mount loomed majestically tall beyond the Ah!nandita Hills, towering into the sky. The steps on the riverbank at the near end, where Zara sat all day, were deserted; the creatures were all gone.

Level III

The Essence of Being

Chapter 1

'Uff! It's going to be such a long journey,' Zara looked at the horizon. It was dawn. The elephant had trudged all night long going around the bend of the Peacock Ridge as she lay on his back. And now, she woke up to the early rays of the sun, her legs dangling behind the elephant's giant ears; Zara sat erect on his shoulders.

From the elevation where they stood, a vast forest canopy unfolded before their eyes, far, far beyond which lay miles upon miles of a vast mustard field splashed in a sea of yellow and green, enclosed by the sweeping arc of the river, now a gigantic flow of mud, flanked by the metro, a distant shimmering blotch on its far bank.

'I could take the shortcut, but that's a dangerous downhill climb, Zara. I have to watch my weight. When I was a kid, my mama told me to take the well-trodden path. It's best that way,' the elephant said, trudging down the slope.

'You are too cautious, Elly,' Zara chided him. A cool breeze wafted in, caressing her face.

'How exhilarating,' Zara exclaimed, her face moistened by the mist brought along by the breeze.

'Hi Zaru!' the breeze wished her. 'I am the west

wind that rose from the ocean. And now, I am on my way to the mountain where the river is born.'

'Oh! I see. So, you carry the river in you? Why, you sure are Rivah! How I have been missing you since I left your bank.'

The west wind laughed, 'Call me whateva you will, Jo tu hai, so main hoon . . .'

'Jo main hoon, so tu hai,' giggled Zara.

And the west wind wrapped herself around Zara.

'I can see you are headed to where the sun sets each day. Way to go,' she said.

'I know. My future beckons me there. But isn't it too far, Windy dear?' asked Zara, almost complaining.

'The mind is there to weaken you, young lady. It's important to confirm your beliefs before you embark on such a long journey. You have to motivate yourself, Zaru. Just be,' the west wind said.

'And how do I do that?' Zara asked, worry furrowing a deep groove on her forehead.

'The traveller lives in the moment,' the west wind went on.

'There is no past, no future. Live here and now. That's how you motivate yourself on such an arduous journey through life, Zaru.'

'Sounds cool,' replied Zara, perking up. 'You're lotsa fun, dear Windy.'

The west wind laughed, 'We all need fun, Zaru.'

'What's the point withdrawing into the unknown? Even the invisible needs visibility for the sake of fun. That's how I become the river,' she continued.

'Yes, that's how I, too, am leaving my unknown world by the river and heading for the known Universe instead, under the glare of city lights,' said Zara, matter-of-factly.

'That's great. The foothills were only an escape from the mundane,' the west wind came back.

'All the creatures you met by the riverbank have since returned to the city to participate in their daily grind and find their bearings. Go, give it a try. Who knows what you will come up with once you reach your station.'

Zara smiled, thanked the west wind, and invited her to join her on the journey beyond.

'There's nothing up there on the mountaintop. It's barren,' she said, prodding the elephant behind its ears to move forward.

The west wind smiled, then turned about and wrapped herself around Zara once more, whispering softly into her ear, 'Don't worry, dear. I'll always come back. But you must keep moving on,' and saying so, she disappeared nowhere with a whoosh.

The elephant trundled towards the plains below. And they rambled till they were swallowed by an ocean of darkness, the shadow of the Peacock Ridge looming large from behind. The city sparkled in the distant horizon in the dazzle of a million neon lights in rows after rows of semi-circular grids laid out one after another.

'Those gemstones . . . they are so beautiful!' exclaimed Zara, drawing a deep breath at the sight of the city still far, far away.

'Yes, they look great, Zara, to the untrained eye, chasing a dream as you do now,' said the elephant. 'But look again. We spend a lifetime propping up concepts that aren't really true.'

'Really?' wondered Zara with a hint of sarcasm.

'Truth, Zara,' said the elephant winking, 'is that that is invariant in all frames of reference. Just like me.'

'To the creature with limited vision, I might appear, at once, a log; at others, a pillar or two or four; sometimes, a rope or even a barrel. But to the one with complete vision, I am what I really am, an elephant.'

'Hmmm!' Zara reflected, yawning.

'Those are city lights you see in the distance that switch on as darkness descends upon our world,' said the elephant.

And so, he trundled along . . .

In a moment, all was quiet.

Chapter 2

When morning came again, the elephant had descended to the plains, the Peacock Ridge towering right behind. At its feet, a shallow stream wound its way into the surrounding wilderness.

Zara looked up. Tall green grasses grew across the stream beyond which tall dark trees merged into a dense forest. Slowly, one at a time, the elephant dipped his feet in the ankle-deep water to make his way to the opposite bank.

'What you see across is elephant grass. They are taller than me. Luscious. I feed on them whenever I get a chance,' the elephant said. Soon, they were wading through the grass, sharp blades slicing into Zara's tender skin.

'Uff!' screamed Zara.

'Mind yourself,' the elephant hollered. 'Don't fling your arms around. And try to hide your legs behind my ears, as much as you can.'

Zara crouched over the elephant's head, shutting her eyes. Soon, they were lost in the dense foliage. An intoxicating sweet smell of rich grass and damp earth filled her nostrils. The *koel* sang aloud from her nest in the trees:

How would I know, O Lord!
What's good for me?
The wise one
Dwelling within
Please show me the way.

'Who's that?' Zara asked.

'That's the koel with the most beautiful voice in all of creation. Few in the forest can see her around, though everybody is well-tuned into her voice. I'd love to sing one day,' the elephant said.

'You are what you hear, dear Elly. Rest easy!' said Zara.

'I like that,' said the elephant, laughing aloud and blowing his trumpet. 'I feel soooo happy.'

And the west wind reappeared from nowhere. 'I see you bruised all over, Zaru, let me heal them with my kiss.' And so, she wrapped herself around Zara, caressing her face.

'Ouch! It hurts,' Zara cried aloud at the touch of the wind. And the wind stepped back.

'Pain and gain belong to the same wheel of life. Don't get taken in by your words,' she said, consoling Zara. And then, looking the elephant in his eyes as he stepped on to a small meadow separating the treeline, she said, 'Surrender yourself to your voice within. That's the lord of your destiny, dear Elly. That's what the koel was singing about.'

'Within, without, within, without. *Cooh . . . cooh*,' the koel sang in her nest. And the birds in the forest joined in:

Cooh . . . cooh!
Hear the sound of
Joy and happiness
In the silence
Of your heart . . .

'Listen carefully, Zaru,' the west wind came around to the elephant's shoulder. 'The birds understand what I mean. You really have to reach nowhere to be truly happy. Be still. Be content with what you have in every situation. And you will feel happy. That's bliss!'

And the birds continued singing:

Cooh . . . cooh!
Hear the sound of
Joy and happiness
In the silence
Of your heart . . .

And the sun peered into the forest in a thousand rays streaming between the trees.

And Zara smiled.

'Bliss? I've heard that one before . . . on the riverbank. Who was it who told me so?' she tried to recall. And she thought and thought and thought.

'Ah yes! Now I remember. It was Anty. He lectured me on motion one day.'

'Motion? Movement creates tension, tension creates anxiety, anxiety causes pain. Remember!' said the west wind. 'There's true bliss when there is stability within. When everything inside is quiet.'

'That's funny. And it's quite impossible for me not to move, just as it is with you, O Windy! How do I get that?' asked Zara.

'I'll tell you how. The trick is to live in cheer,' the wind laughed aloud.

'Cheer? But, I am always smiling, am I not?' Zara asked.

'Sure, you are. But you need to paste a permanent smile on that face.'

'Emojis, you mean?' winked Zara.

'Yes, you get three of a kind,' the west wind laughed back.

'Whew! Three cheers to that,' yelled Zara.

'Hurrah!' came a voice from the forest across the meadow. Zara looked up, surprised.

It was the monkey, hanging by its tail from the tree. And shortly, all the other monkeys joined in, hanging from nearby branches.

'Hurrah! Hurrah! Hurrah!' they screamed, jumping from branch to branch.

'Great to see you guys around. Now listen to what I say . . .'

'Carry on Windy, we are all ears,' the monkeys responded in one loud chatter.

'First is the cheer of the body. Elly knows that well.' And the elephant nodded in agreement. 'A full smiley comes with wholesome food,' the wind carried on.

'Yeah, yeah!' nodded the elephant. 'I feed on rich

green grass. But if you eat like the pig . . .' he said, pointing his trunk to the wild hog sitting by a pile of waste in the slush to the far left of the meadow, feeding on rot, '. . . you will stink like a sack full of garbage and always remain disgruntled.'

'So, don't be in a hurry to hog,' the west wind turned around. 'Don't go against your bodily nature. To know how and what suits you best, first sniff like a dog.'

'*Bow-wow*!' Pleased by the praise, the wild cur barked from behind the woods to the elephant's right, where he had been lazing in the morning sun.

'But he barks unnecessarily,' complained Zara.

'Right? If you really look at it that way, nobody's quite perfect. It's actually quite difficult to keep your mouth shut. Try it out yourself,' the monkey shouted, still hanging by his tail.

'And that's because the mouth has two deformities,' said the west wind. 'It keeps eating, and it keeps talking.'

'Eating, talking . . . talking, eating . . . yes! But how do you really shut your mouth?' the monkey asked. 'After all, eating and talking makes us what we really are.'

'Ha!' exclaimed the west wind. 'A healthy body is born of a healthy mind.'

'Come again?' said the hog, irritated midway through his gorging, raising his head in a slant, looking through the corner of his eyes.

'Come again!' he grunted, spoiling for a fight.

'Your mind controls your lusts. Don't sniff around

for rubbish. Control your urge instead. That's what I said. For our mind to be in control, we must strictly stick to form,' the west wind went on. 'But if you keep hogging all the while, as is your wont, you miss out on the small funs of life.'

'I'll do as I please,' grunted the hog, detesting the jibe.

'There's no such thing as "I'll do as I wish". To nourish a healthy body, you need a healthy mind,' smiled the west wind.

'So, that's cheer No. 2 for you,' the elephant said. 'Sounds good! I always try to keep my mind in cheer. That's exactly what makes me gentle despite my frame.'

'Yes, that's exactly what does. And that brings us to cheer No. 3: gentleness of speech. Express your gratitude with every step you take, such that the other person has tears in their eyes.'

'Well said, and three cheers to that!' exclaimed Zara.

'Hurrah! Hurrah! Hurrah!' the monkeys jumped about.

'See ya, then!' the west wind said. 'But remember, if you can't spread cheer, don't pass around your sorrows.'

And saying so, she bid all goodbye.

Chapter 3

It had begun to rain. First, gently, and then, a heavy downpour came calling on the meadow. The west wind rose to the sky, howling furiously. And the rains lashed down upon earth, as if in vengeance, in a violent outburst, as tormenting flashes of lightning rode the sky, and the dark clouds cast their spell, swallowing the sun. The forest fell silent as the rain drenched every soul, Zara and the elephant included.

Zara did not remember seeing such a storm before when she grew up by the riverbank. This, certainly, was different.

Presently, the hog rose, stinking, grunting, plastered in mud, and charged deep inside the forest. And one by one, the monkeys ran helter-skelter.

'What do we do, Elly?' Zara asked.

'Ahem! We are stuck,' the elephant said, almost apologetic about his weight. And they stood wondering by the meadow's edge. The elephant turned around once, looking at the tall green grass. Then turned around once more, now facing the forest that looked dark and foreboding. A puddle started to gather on the meadow, soon blanketing it under a sheet of water.

'What do we do now?' Zara asked again, when a voice interrupted, '*Kitch, kitch, kitch!*'

Zara bent on the elephant's back, looking to the ground near his feet. It was the monkey.

'Hi! What brings you here?' Zara asked, her mouth agape, engaging an ape for the first time ever.

'Hi, Zara! I am Monk!ee. I belong to the forest,' he said, jumping up to the elephant's shoulder, right next to Zara.

'O Monk!ee, tell us fast what to do. It's quite damp and cold out here in the open,' Zara snapped.

'Yup! Sure it is. But it's fun, too,' replied the monkey. 'If I wanna hide from this rain, I really need to dig deep under the rock, but the fun is not in my being able to chart my own path and move ahead alone. The fun is in being able to do it while taking everybody along,' the monkey said at the speed of a hurricane in a single breath, flashing his teeth.

'Yeah! I understand,' screamed Zara. 'Now do it and show us the way.'

'Sure, I will,' said the monkey. 'When you reach the city, you will be greeted by a graffiti that says, "Greater the challenge, greater the excitement." Come, it's time for an adventure.'

'You sure are having fun, while I am drenched to my bones,' Zara shouted back.

'Yeah, keep playing the game, Zara. Make the best of it while it lasts,' the monkey said. 'Every day is a new day. Every day you gift yourself a new world, Zara.'

'It beats me how? I didn't quite ask for this,' Zara shouted. 'I'm so wet . . . and disgusted.'

'Think again, Zara,' the elephant interrupted. 'You asked me to the city. So, here we are.'

Zara, visibly irritated, shouted back, 'Guy! You sure have a way with words. I asked for the city, not the jungle.'

'The way to "the good life" is through the jungle of the mind. Zara, you have to walk through the forest to reach the city one day,' the elephant shot back, smiling.

Zara raised her face to the tormented sky, slapped her forehead and cried, 'Good Lord! Now cut the crap. Why did I have to ask for this?'

In the distance inside the forest, the storm raged hard and the wind creaked through the hollow, and then, a giant tree came crashing with a thud, shaking the ground. Even the elephant trembled.

'Never blame yourself Zara,' the monkey came back from his momentary distraction, scratching his head. 'Never lose faith in yourself. You are the best that could ever happen to your Universe, Zara,' he said.

'But what exactly brings me here?' Zara asked. 'Why do I have to trample through a storm-wracked forest to reach my destination? Isn't this an unnecessary diversion?'

'It's the way you look at life. Tell yourself, Zara, that you are here to revel in the wonder that comes from the abundance of nature. Take a good look around. The thunderstorm is gone. There is simply no sorrow, no disgust for you when you chart your life's destination,' said the monkey.

It was calm once more as a pleasant quiet descended upon the forest. The earth was soaked in water, the leaves and branches and the tall grass heavily drenched in the rain. Slowly, but certainly, the sun winked from behind the clouds, their dark and menacing demeanour making way for giant silvery-white puffs in a westward drift. The west wind crept back upon the meadow, with a gentle chill. Whistling!

The koel caught the drift of the whistle. Then shaking her throat clear, she sang:

Oh mind, don't ask
Of the
Hows and whys,
Your voice will guide you
Outta darkness one day.

And all the other birds of the forest joined in chorus:

Your voice will guide you
Outta darkness one day.

'The trick, Zaru,' the west wind said, going down, prodding the elephant's ankle, 'is to walk one step at a time, upright and honest. There has to be integrity in every step you take.'

The elephant raised his trunk and blew his trumpet, very pleased with himself. Then, one foot at a time, he moved forward across the meadow, towards the forest, leaving giant footprints in the mud.

'That's a good way to go, Elly,' the west wind said, and then, rising with a whoosh to where Zara sat on the elephant's shoulders, she whispered into her ear, 'Be normal. Be natural. Keep courage. The storm is over. Once the image is gone, it's the end of story. Change your mind every day, Zaru.'

'As ifff . . .' Zara dragged herself, taunt painted on her lips. 'Can't you feel I am wet and lonely? And the jungle looks so scary. Whateva brought me here?'

'What's done is done,' the west wind said. 'There's little point talking irrelevant stuff now that you are here. Be Aware. Have Patience. Practice. That's "app" for you, Zaru.'

'Get it?' the elephant asked Zara, forcing his pace towards the forest through the slush. 'Be what you are. Be Aware. Have Patience. Practice. And the biggest storm shall pass over. I am, Zara, what I am. Just be! For app's the nature of the beast.'

Chapter 4

Evening set in by the time the elephant crossed the meadow and stood at the edge of the forest, his feet heavily sodden.

The sun had gone down behind the Peacock Ridge, now standing like a dark sentinel in the distance, overlooking the elephant grass, the stream, the meadow, and the jungle; the faint rays of the setting sun painting the western sky in scarlet hues on a dark canvas.

The crickets chirped aloud in the cover of the trees, now dark and deep and lonely. The elephant raised his trunk, blowing his trumpet, signalling the creatures of the forest to make way.

Zara's heart pounded against her chest, *thud . . . thud . . . thud,* and then, she felt a gentle breeze flowing from the meadow, caressing her back.

'Windy?' she enquired softly, turning her head around.

'Yes, Zaru, do not be afraid,' the west wind said. 'Be quiet. Be gentle.'

'Yes,' Zara whispered.

'You have to cross the forest to reach the city. So, get across, no matter what comes your way.'

'I know . . .'

'Make the best use of what you have while you are here. The forest teaches us several things, Zaru, in our journey through life on this earth.'

'But above all, it teaches us to let be. The forest is home to many creatures, big and small. And they do not come your way, unless, of course, you are game. It's important, Zaru, to kill your ego inside and move forward with a humble heart. Then, and then alone, will you shed your fear.'

'I understand,' declared Zara. 'But my heart keeps pounding, Windy. I need to calm down.'

'Never mind the heartbeat, Zaru. Storms are meant to bring calm after the tormenting summer heat,' the west wind said.

'It's going to be disgraceful, Windy, if I can't make it to the city,' Zara said, tears welling up her eyes. 'I created such a fuss to get there,' she said, wiping her forehead, sweating with nervous tension.

'Nervousness got nobody nowhere, O Zaru!' the west wind said. 'So, do not be tormented by your mind. Let the forest consume you if it will. All you must do is be a witness to your thoughts as you go along. Life will carry on.'

'How are you so cocksure, Windy?' Zara asked.

'I say from experience. When the sun vaporises the river, the river reappears in a million drops of rain. So it is with you and me. This, too, shall pass.'

'Hey baby, you're getting heavy on me,' the elephant interrupted, shaking Zara with his laughter. 'Be light of being.'

And saying so, he walked into the darkness. The chirping of crickets grew louder and louder.

Chapter 5

It must have been quite a long trek in the dark through the undergrowth and thickets when the elephant suddenly stopped in his tracks, confronted by a pair of bloodshot phosphorescent eyes glowing in the distance.

'Hehehe, I am the hyena,' came a voice from the other end. 'I am the gatekeeper to the forest.'

'You . . . sure . . . are . . .' yawned Zara, carelessly rubbing her eyes. 'I can see you will show us the way as the monkey did when we first arrived on the edge of the forest.'

'That's well said, Zara,' the hyena came back. 'I can see you are already beginning to shed your fear. Your fear comes from your thoughts, dear friend.'

'Lemme think that through,' Zara said, looking the hyena in the eye. 'But first, I need to wake up from my slumber.' And saying so, Zara stretched her arms.

'Take your time, young lady,' the hyena said. And then, he took off:

> There are three types of thoughts that engage the mind. The first happens when we remember unnecessary scenes from our past, distorting our perspective of life.

'The other, of course, is influenced by what we see around. And what we see may not be what we really desire.'

'And then, there is the third kind. And that comes from the power of our knowledge. Wise travellers use their knowledge to read the past and interpret what they see around to chart their future path.'

'Zara, be a witness to your thoughts. Figure out how the elephant leads you out of the jungle.'

'Well said, Redeyes, thank you for that compliment,' the elephant said.

'You are welcome,' said the hyena. 'Remember, Zara, the forest is irrelevant to your journey. You have to tackle the trees that stand in your way, instead. Your desire to reach the city must not get distorted by your fear, or else, you will lose yourself trapped in the forest, unable to reach your journey's end.'

'You are wise,' said Zara. 'Even Windy told me so. But tell me, Redeyes, how do you do that?'

'I will, Zara,' said the hyena, looking Zara in the eye. 'But first, I must ask what's taking you to the city?'

'Oh! That's not a big deal,' said Zara. 'As a child, I perceived the glow of city lights in the night sky, far, far beyond the Peacock Ridge. And ever since, all the creatures by the riverbank told me that my life as a human is best lived under the glare of the neon. So, here I am, on my way to where I must belong.'

'Aha!' exclaimed the hyena. 'I see. Then I'll stop you no more. But, Zara, you should know where your craving comes from.'

And saying so, the hyena broke into a hymn:

Thoughts lead to affirmation,
Affirmation to desire,
Desire leads to thirst,
Thirst to craving.

And then, raising his voice, he said, 'The trick is to achieve without action, to speak without a word.'

'Will that give me satisfaction, Redeyes?' Zara asked.

'Satisfaction, Zara,' said the hyena, 'is that that fulfils my need. Whateva else I achieve, I do with a clear understanding that I am only playing a game.'

'The reason why we are unhappy is the non-performance, nonachievement, non-fulfilment of our desires. There is no satisfaction where you are seeking satisfaction, Zara.'

'Zara,' interrupted the elephant, excited. 'We spend a lifetime chasing our desires. For you, it may well be the glare of the neon lights, like the flame is to the moth. But remember, dear, we seldom enjoy what we already have. Make the best of this adventure in the wild while we roam the jungle.'

And the forest fell silent.

***

Zara was about to return to her sleep when a rustle in the undergrowth woke her up.

'Now, who's that?' she shouted disapprovingly.

'It's the rhino on his way back home, Zara,' said the elephant. 'He hurts no one.'

'Yeah, it's me,' the rhino cried out, brushing past the elephant.

And then, apologetically, he said, 'You've already heard a lot Zara, it's time to get some sleep. Sorry to have disturbed you, darling.'

'Access control, again? Oh! Thank you. I can sure do with some rest, gatekeeper,' Zara replied, her eyes narrowing.

'Ha, ha! I have just one last word for you, though,' said the rhino.

'Remembah, whateva you do, whereva you go, you do it for your own good. Revel in the creation of your Universe. Live in exuberance, Zara.'

'That's well said, Rhi!noo. I really like that,' replied Zara. 'I am the creator of my Universe indeed. That's for certain.'

'Yeah, yeah! Believe, believe, believe, believe! Believe yourself, Zara. Believe your voice within,' said the rhino, pushing into the thick foliage on his path.

And then, wishing Zara goodnight, he said, 'Nobody wants to dwell in his dream foreva . . . nobody wants to keep chasing an illusion. If you look at it deeply, everybody wants just enough to be happy. That's what you are meant to be, dear.'

Chapter 6

Zara woke up under the green canopy of the forest rambling atop the elephant. Soon, they came to the rhino, feeding on the foliage in a clearing.

'Who's that?' Zara asked the elephant, bending down to his ears.

'That's the rhino who brushed past us last night, Zara,' the elephant said.

'Oh yes,' said Zara. 'I didn't get to see him in the dark. Isn't he huge and strong?'

'He sure is,' said the elephant, smiling, 'but not quite as huge as . . .'

'I know, I know,' said Zara. 'You are the greatest evah!'

The rhino caught Zara's last words, looking up midcourse through his morning meal. And he smiled, 'Good morning, Zara.'

'A very good morning to you,' replied Zara. 'You look handsome, dear Rhi!noo.'

The rhino let out a big laugh and asked Zara where she was off to early in the morning.

'To the city, of course. It's a long way off,' said Zara.

'The city?' asked the rhino. 'And where are you coming from?'

'From the river's lap beyond the Peacock Ridge.'

'Rivah!? Peacock Ridge?' the rhino wondered aloud, looking suspicious.

'Yes, that mountain behind the forest. That's the Peaco . . . Why . . . ? Just a moment!' And then, turning around towards the mountain, her jaw fell.

'Why? From this side of the mountain face, there's really no peacock. It's just like any other mountain,' Zara said, cupping her mouth with her palm.

She turned to the elephant, surprised to ask what had become of the gemstones atop the mountain, strung together in the shape of the bejewelled peacock.

The wise elephant who had roamed the earth, nodded his head, swaying his trunk from left to right and right to left.

And he said, 'O Zara! The bejewelled peacock you saw atop the mountain at night while you grew up by the riverbank was a figment of your imagination, luring you all these years in the direction of the city. But now that you have moved on in life, and stand where you are today, it's just another mountain from your past. Come to think of it, Zara, you come here to the forest on your way to the city not from the river, which, again, is your past imagination, but from the bottom of the valley at the mouth of the glacier, high up in the mountains, riding the water, playing with the wind.'

'Bottom? High? Water? Wind?' Zara looked askance, 'Valley? Glacier? Mountain? Forest? City?'

'The cycle of life, Zara,' said the rhino. 'There is no start, no finish. Just understand the context to which you belong. And that context is here and now.'

'Is it all an illusion? Really!' exclaimed Zara, wondering.

'Oh yes, it is. Life itself is an illusion, Zara,' the rhino said. 'But we do not wish to live by the illusion of life. All we seek and desire is to live happily evah aftah.'

'How true,' said Zara. And then, she set about thinking, 'Why do we crave to be happy?'

'Good question,' said the rhino. 'Do you know why I wear a thick hide?'

'No,' said Zara.

'It's because this life is a constant war that nobody wants to lose,' said the rhino. 'We all need to win our wars, whateva the cost, in order to survive this journey through the forest of life, either by surrendering our ego or by grabbing the other person's collar.'

'To live life, Zara, is an art. Learn to negotiate your life. The moment you forget what's good for your survival, you fight, and you hurt your cause. So, it's best to wear a thick skin in your journey through life,' the rhino said.

'Nobody does anything for anybody, Zara,' the elephant interrupted. 'Everybody does everything for their own happiness. They do it for their own bliss.'

The leaves rustled in the wind . . . and the birds twittered . . . and the monkeys chattered . . . taken by the wisdom of the rhino. Zara blew a goodbye kiss at him and, one step at a time, the elephant walked away.

And as the elephant walked the track into the bushes, the west wind reappeared from nowhere.

'Your life's already on track, Zaru. The day you get the signal, you will move ahead, as you did from the river's bank. Go deep into the woods of your mind, Zaru, to figure out what you want.'

'It's going to be a long journey!' Zara said, half a smile pasted on her lips, half a worry furrowed on her forehead.

'Strengthen yourself so much that you can take care of yourself.'

'How?' Zara asked.

'Get the rubbish outta your mind. Just empty yourself within.'

'That's easier said than done,' Zara mocked. 'My will to carry on is failing me.'

'Why do you say that?' the west wind asked. 'Just rise above your weakness. Give yourself a push. Push your desires hard, Zaru. Heave-ho!'

'Easier said than done, Windy. I feel tired and lonesome.'

'Easier said than done?' the west wind laughed. 'Do what you must to get to the city. Be of use to yourself. The rest is irrelevant. Just believe in yourself. Believe in your love for life. And finally, you will get there one day.'

'You think so?' Zara asked.

'Know yourself, Zaru. Understand yourself. Be in the forest as you are now, for as long as it takes, but don't get involved. Have patience.'

'All you need, Zaru, is a firm belief in where you wish to be. You have to really do nothing else.'

'The end is already good. The end really is the beginning.'

And saying so, the west wind blew away.

Chapter 7

At noon, the elephant suggested a break. He had been walking days and nights on end when they reached a pond, its surface covered by round, green hyacinth leaves. The elephant halted, then bent down on the water's edge for Zara to get off his back. Zara jumped down, then loitered around to the far end of the pond and sat in the shade of an old banyan tree.

'Aha! Finally, some rest,' the elephant said, raising his trunk, yawning.

'Care for a swim, Zara? It's been a long time,' he asked.

'That would be nice. Come, let's make a splash,' Zara said, jumping up for some action.

'In a while,' said the elephant. 'First, let me catch my breath. Meanwhile, take a look around this place. It's interesting.' And saying so, he rolled over in the mud.

Zara, too, stretched her tallish frame under the banyan and looked up at its hanging roots, intertwined with one another. The tree must have been standing wise and tall for many, many years, she thought.

'You are off to the city, aren't you, Zara?' the banyan asked gently. '. . . to live out the city life?'

'Oh yeah! I am headed that way. It's gonna be one

helluva fun. How long have you been around?' Zara asked.

'Must have been many, many moons ago,' the banyan said. 'I have lost count. It looks like eternity . . .' he said, losing himself in deep thought.

And then, he said with a shrug, 'Now come to think of it, I remember there was a city here once upon a time, long, long ago. That was much before the forest crept over and the creatures moved in. If you look around this place, you might still find a few ruins, here and there, inhabited by the monkeys.'

'Really?' Zara jumped up excited. 'How marvellous! The jungle stands where a city stood once? You mean it?'

'Yes, Zara, it's true. That's the nature of life. Growth gives way to decay. And out of decay, new life is born,' said the banyan.

'How sad. What could have happened to all those people who lived in this city? I feel sorry for them,' Zara said, anguish crawling to life on her face.

'Do not waste your emotions, Zara,' the banyan said.

'Your sorrow comes from within. Solve your sorrows within. Remember, there is no joy in the material things of life. The treasure lies buried someplace else.'

And saying so, the banyan broke into a song in his sonorous voice:

> Wheneva I chased joy,
> I drowned myself in tears . . .

'Why's that so?' Zara asked.

'It's because of what we do. Do, but without arrogance, Zara. And there will be little reason to cry,' said the banyan.

Zara lay there, stretched out, one leg crossed over the other. Looking up at the branches and the aerial roots where the birds had woven their nests in corners and crevices. And the hours passed by . . .

The elephant yawned and then, rose with a shrug at the opposite end of the pond from where Zara lay resting in the banyan's shade.

'Come on, Zara, let's have some fun,' he cried out, loudly blowing his trumpet. And saying so, he descended into the pond with a big splash before pushing through the hyacinth. Zara stood up, shrugged herself, and dived into the water at the far side.

'Oops!' she yelled, rising to the surface. 'I am getting entangled in these shoots and leaves. Elly, let's see who reaches the centre first.' And saying so, she pushed aside the hyacinth, stroking the water with her arms and legs, moving forward.

'I'll get there first,' the elephant shouted, ploughing into the weeds, sucking in water through his trunk, and spraying a fountain in the sky.

The sun watched from above and smiled. The banyan swayed with laughter. And watching them make merry, Zara flailed her arms more vigorously.

'There's bliss neither in knowledge nor in dedication. What's there is there in you. Enjoy the moment.'

Saying so, the west wind gently swooped down to the water's surface where Zara swam.

'You here, too?' Zara looked up. 'I feel so good and refreshed.'

'Yes, we are all here to celebrate your twenty-second birthday, Zaru,' the west wind said. 'Look around. Not a single soul in this forest is perfect. Some can run, others can fly, while others can jump or swim. But we all are here together to make the forest what it really is. Be part of the bouquet, Zara.'

'Bouquet? What's that?' Zara asked, looking around for a clue.

The forest was awash in colours. All its animals—the monkeys, the hog, the hyena, the rhino, and the deer—were gathered by the pond. And so were all the birds. The water lilies and lotuses in white and cream and yellow and pink danced in full bloom. Watching Zara and the elephant revelling in water, furrowing through the hyacinth, as they coursed towards each other. And all of creation revelled at the sight of the playmates making a splash.

'A bouquet, Zaru,' the west wind said, 'is a clutch of flowers standing cheerfully together in one tight grip, sharing the colours of creation with one and all. It's one in many and many in one.'

'I understand. Like the forest,' Zara smiled.

And the west wind laughed, rushing up, flinging her arms over the forest cover, gathering an abundance of flowers of various hues and scents in her mighty embrace, and then, she littered them all over the pond, above the floating carpet of green formed by the hyacinth leaves.

And she sang, 'Happy birthday, Zaru . . .'

And the entire forest came alive in a chorus, 'A hap-happy birthday to you.'

And, in that merry moment, the elephant blew his trumpet. Then, noticed by none, he suddenly started sliding into the pond; his huge frame beginning to sink out of sight. Startled, he shouted for help.

'Oooh! Heeeeeeeeeelp! Help me, Zara,' he cried in desperation, raising his trunk skywards, his head still above water, as he went slipping . . . slipping . . . slipping.

'Heeelp!' Zara shouted. 'Somebody please help Elly!' she cried in panic, realising the crisis at hand, but not knowing what had taken the elephant. And cutting through the hyacinth, she made a desperate dash for her friend.

'I am sinking, Zara, in a quagmire. It's time for me to go,' the elephant cried, tears welling up in his eyes, sinking, his trunk still raised to the sky.

'Hold on!' Zara shouted. 'What's that? The quagmire? I am on my way to you.'

In all these years, Zara had grown up by the river, things had always appeared the same. The creatures, the crawlies, and the elephant. Even the animals of the forest appeared at ease in the days she had wandered around the jungle. So, where were things headed now? she wondered.

Zara and Elly had been around since Zara's bubble

burst on the dry river bed on a hot summer day, when she crawled to the pool that had once been a river. And at first sight, the elephant appeared a pillar . . . then two . . . then three and four, till Zara came to know him better for who he was, the elephant.

And the elephant had always blown his merry trumpet, standing on the promenade, and had now been walking her through the jungle to the city beyond.

'Elly, just hold on!' Zara cried, freeing herself from the weed that clung on to her. 'I'm on my way.'

'Better make it quick,' the elephant squeaked, his once proud masculine voice going weak. 'I'm beginning to go down.'

And as he said so, he started gulping in water while desperately trying to keep his head afloat.

Zara gave herself one mighty push. Stroking her way towards the elephant. With a few more heaves, she was almost there. The gentle beast, his trunk still protruding above the surface, blew his trumpet in a whimper. Ripples formed where he stood once with his head jutting out of water.

'Haa! I'm here, Elly,' Zara heaved, just as his trunk started sinking, creating a hundred bubbles on the water's surface. 'I'm here, come, hold my hand.'

'No waaaayyyyy! Zaruuuuu,' the west wind forced herself, wrapping Zara in her invisible fold. 'No way.'

Zara, her right arm outstretched towards the elephant, looked back.

'Zaru, it's really time to bid goodbye to Elly. Give up, give up, give up!' said the west wind firmly.

'Why do you say so?' Zara shouted irritated, 'Gosh, Elly, here I am.'

'Zaru, stay out or you, too, will be gone down the quagmire of time,' the west wind warned harshly. 'There comes a moment when you simply have to say no, enough is enough.'

'Why'd you say that? Elly was my best frien' foreva,' Zara frowned.

'I understand that and respect your sentiments, Zaru. But I must also tell you that it's essential for you to experience everything in life, even a sense of loss. You must learn when not to jump the threshold. And this moment is your test of time,' the west wind said.

'But Elly, my BFF? We spent so many wonderful years together,' Zara lamented, splashing her arms about the water, trying to free herself from the west wind's hold.

'We suffer our memories, Zaru, don't we? Don't be weak. Weakness is death. She, and she alone, is a brave soul who can say no,' the west wind said, admonishing Zara for throwing a tantrum.

'A healthy person, Zaru,' the wind went on, 'has all the emotions, all the qualities, but doesn't allow herself to be blackmailed by them. Be alert, Zaru.'

'I don't buy that,' Zara protested. 'I don't buy your argument. Elly was truly a great friend. He never blackmailed me eva . . .'

'Zaru, remember, you came here on way to the city,' the west wind said, now calm. 'The city, not the forest, is your final destination. Go, fulfil your desires first. Be patient to satiate your hunger.'

'But the elephant made me happy,' Zara seemed to argue, now considerably calmed down by the west wind's soothing words.

'That was then, till he went down under the weight of time. This time is yours and yours alone, Zaru.'

Zara stared at the spot where the elephant went down struggling for breath. The water was calm and silent, topped by the hyacinth. For a long, long time, Zara fixed her gaze at that spot thinking and thinking and thinking.

'Be a turtle, Zaru. Use your limbs and emotions at will, and on time. Improve your habits and you will be strong,' the west wind said, caressing Zara's face.

Zara was lost in the memory of time.

'Willing renunciation is the essence of bliss, Zara,' came a soft and soothing voice, as a wizened face, cracked by age, peeped out of the water. For a moment Zara thought the elephant had resurfaced.

'Bliss that comes and never goes away is bliss.'

It was the turtle.

***

That night, as Zara lay under the banyan, resting her head on the turtle lying belly side up, the west wind crept over to Zara. Then kissing her goodnight, she said, 'Don't remain a kid all your life, Zaru, it's time to grow up.'

'What do I do then?' Zara asked, still overcome by grief.

'Just surrender yourself as a log to the will of time and the artisan will sculpt you into shape,' the west wind said before blowing away.

Chapter 8

Zara woke up at dawn to the koel's song:

Your due shall come your way,
Have faith in who you are.
Share whateva you own
Live and let live.

Zara looked up at the branches of the banyan tree. The koel was hiding amidst the leaves. Soon, the other birds joined in:

Your due shall come your way,
Have faith in who you are.
Share whateva you own
Live and let live.

And the banyan's leaves rustled in the wind.

'Good morning, Zara. Slept well?' the turtle asked.

'Yeah, sorta,' Zara replied. 'It's time to get going. I have to reach the city.'

'How do you distinguish between what's true and what's not?' the west wind swept down the branches where she had been humming with the birds.

'How?' Zara asked.

'Ask your voice within,' said the west wind. 'It's your lonesome voice that tells you what's yours and what's not.'

'But how do I recognise my voice within? It could well be yours instead,' Zara said, still lying down, her head resting on the turtle's stomach.

'Wait till you reach the city and you will get to learn,' the west wind said. 'Those neon lights you have seen from the heights of the Peacock Ridge . . .'

'The city! Ah! The city lights,' said Zara. 'The glow of the neon entices me from afar.'

'Do you know what makes them glow?' asked the west wind.

'No,' replied Zara.

'That glow comes from the power within. You don't need to touch the power to feel its glow. It's there. Period. And you realise that out of realisation.'

'Sounds complicated,' Zara said. 'I've realised nothing of that kind.'

'I can see your fantasies make you happy . . .' the west wind said.

Zara interrupted, 'Yes, they do.'

'. . . but they will never satisfy you, Zaru,' the west wind continued.

'What will, then?' Zara got up to catch the wind in the face.

'Your satisfaction comes from giving your heart out, Zaru,' the west wind said.

'Like Elly's?' Zara asked.

'Yes, and more. When you walk with your voice till

the end, without seeking anything, you will only give. Give, but do not take, Zaru.'

'I have nothing to give,' Zara smiled. 'I came here with nothing . . . on the elephant's back . . .'

'. . . but your imagination and your voice,' the turtle joined in.

'Yeah. So, make the best use of what you have. Face every situation, Zara. But use the power of your voice within and your judgment to get what you desire,' said the wise ol' turtle.

'Learn to distinguish between what's true and what's not, Zaru,' the west wind said.

Zara sat pensive. Thinking. Thinking deep. 'What's true? What's untrue . . . ?' she wondered.

'True?' she asked herself again, raising a brow. 'Untrue.' And she looked into the pond where the elephant had gone down.

'There's hyacinth there . . . that's true?' she asked herself. Then, she replied, 'No . . . there's water there? That's true?'

'Where's the water?' asked the turtle, testing Zara.

'There's only the hyacinth where you look. That's the truth.'

Zara paused, and thought and thought and thought. And then, slowly raising her voice, she said, 'There's only truth.'

'Only truth?' asked the turtle, now raising his brow.

'Only truth?' asked the west wind, smirk scribbled on her face.

'Only truth!' said Zara. 'There's no untruth. What

is, is true. Also, what is under the hyacinth is the other truth. So, what we often get to see is the half-truth, and then, there is also a second choice. There is only truth. There is no other.'

'You are right, Zaru,' the west wind clapped. 'There is the moon. You only get to see its one side. But there are two faces of the moon. Still, it is the moon.'

The turtle rolled over to stand up on its feet. 'It's like me, Zara. What you get to see is the truth. From the top, you get to see my hard side, hard like the rock. Turn me around, and you get to see my soft underbelly that hurts when you hit me hard.'

'Really! Really! Reaaaaally!' Zara exclaimed, her eyes gleaming.

And the west wind smiled. 'You got it, Zaru.'

'I got it!' Zara exclaimed.

'Now, you won't quite get to explore the dark side of the moon, Zaru, but if you do get to see the dark side, don't feel scared.'

Chapter 9

Zara had sheltered herself under the banyan tree for several nights, her hair growing longer, not knowing which way to head. She never expected to figure her way out of the jungle as long as the elephant was around. But now, she was on her own, lost and lonely, overcome by grief ever since Elly went down under, sinking in the pond.

Yes, the west wind always came around whenever Zara needed her the most, but she could certainly not ride the wind to the city, that lay far away to the west, as she had surfed the water, from the glacier's tongue to the riverbank 276 full moons ago.

True, the giant turtle was always around at hand, but Zara never imagined that she could ride him to the city. So, she stayed under the banyan, taking in the marvels of the forest, chatting up its inhabitants, figuring out whom to count on to show her the way out.

And the moon waxed and waned, and the seasons passed by, returning at regular intervals. And the summer heat made way for torrential rains, the rains made way for mellow autumn that made way for mild winter, which, in turn, made way for severe cold, and severe cold made way for bright spring—when the trees dressed up in fresh green coats—and the forest came alive in the shades of rainbow pastels of orange and green and violet and yellow flowers. And the birds came back singing to the forest after their winter recess. And the pleasant sunshine poured down to the forest floor once more where dead leaves shed by the trees in winter rustled under the trample of Zara's feet and those of other animals.

And as with most other creatures, the forest became home to Zara as she wandered around from tree to tree, chatting up the animals and birds.

Still, the lure of the city remained as Zara wondered if she would ever find her way out when, one bright morning, the koel sang:

> You are weak, he is strong,
> Every friendship has a purpose.
> Don't fall in love . . .

'Don't fall in love . . . in love . . . in love . . .' the other birds joined in.

'In love . . . in love . . . in love,' Zara, too, joined them.

'Don't fall in love . . .' the koel sang.

'You are weak, he is strong,

Is strong . . . is strong . . . is strong,' the other birds sang.

'Every friendship has a purpose . . . a purpose . . . a purpose,' Zara joined the chorus.

And the west wind blew in, sweeping the forest

floor, driving the dry leaves around from here to there and from there to here.

'Retain your freedom, Zaru,' the west wind said. Don't rest your mind on the objects around . . . on the body . . . on the person. Unshackle yourself, Zaru, lose your sense of the body.'

'Come clear,' Zara told the west wind, raising her voice above the din created by the rustling of leaves on the forest floor.

'Look at the trees, Zaru, they never mourn the loss of their dead leaves, they just let them fall. Never mourn the loss of the body, object, or person, but take good care of all things while they last. Have fun, Zaru, but never possess whateva you consider your own.'

Zara heard out the west wind and looked up at the branches to catch a glimpse of the koel. When she couldn't find her, she turned to the west wind, and asked, 'Windy, where's the koel gone? She sings so well. And she's foreva free. I can sense that in her voice.'

'Yes, she's entirely free, Zaru. And that freedom gives her such a lovely voice. If you hear them well, Zaru, no two birds in the forest sing the same. Each has her distinct voice. And yet, they all sing well because they all are free.'

'Not all the birds, Windy. Certainly not the peacock. It looks so good, but it's got a lousy voice, *kaw . . . kaw . . . kaw*,' Zara said, strutting about like a peacock,

'That's because the peacock is not free, Zaru. He's

trapped in the image of his own beauty to be really free.'

'So, how does one get free, Windy?' Zara asked.

'Aha! You really wish to know?' the west wind asked back.

'Really!' said Zara.

'Well, well, well, the secret to the freedom is not to be a scatterbrain. Freedom demands a lot of patience and focus. The secret to freedom, Zaru, is to resolve to be free. The secret to freedom, Zaru, is to be able to break the rule book only when the situation so demands. Break the rule, Zaru, to be free. And don't get affected by it. That's the secret to freedom.'

'I see, Windy, the secret to freedom lies in the chance you take,' Zara said.

'That's more like it, Zaru,' the west wind came back. 'The seeker is forever in search of an opportunity. Sadly, when that opportunity comes knocking, most don't pick it up.'

'And how does one really pick up a chance?' Zara asked the west wind.

'Just empty yourself within. Never be neither here nor there. Be either here or there. Be either in the city or the forest. Don't keep standing at the crossroads foreva. That, Zaru, is the essence of being. So, give yourself a push to pick up your chance. And soon, you'll be outside the forest.'

'Thank you, Windy,' Zara said. She took one last long look at the pond where the elephant had gone down. And finally, blowing a thank you kiss to the banyan, Zara embarked on her arduous journey beyond.

The west wind smiled, hugged Zara, and leading her out through the thicket, said, 'Come, I'll join you some distance. Don't be too careful, Zara, but don't be too careless either. The time has come for you to leave the forest and head for the city, don't change your belief this time.'

Zara stretched out her hand in the direction of the wind, as if holding her hand out to her to be led out of the undergrowth, as she cleared her path with her other arm, her smile, finally back on her face.

Looking at her, the west wind said, 'That's good. You look cheerful again. Practice equanimity, Zaru, and don't harbour a doubt.'

In a moment, Zara was enveloped by the jungle.

Chapter 10

Late that night, as Zara followed the west wind through the long and unending forest, thorns biting into her skin, she stopped for a moment, tugging the west wind by her hand, and looked back in the direction of the banyan and the pond.

It was pitch dark.

'Is it wrong, Windy, to fall in love?' Zara asked, images of her desperate dash to save the elephant flashing through her mind.

'Keep looking, Zaru,' the west wind said in a calm, collected manner. 'Love others as you would love yourself. But delink your emotions from physical attachment.'

'The elephant, Windy,' said Zara, tears rolling down her cheeks. 'I miss Elly very much, just as I would miss you if you were to leave me now.'

'Zaru, know this well,' the west wind said. 'The basis of all existence is love. Do not judge, just love. And do not live in doubt.'

'I do not live in doubt. It's just that Elly and I grew up together.'

'What's the use of past, Zaru? The past is dead. As for what will happen tomorrow, if I were gone? Well, nobody really has seen the future . . .'

'Live in the present, Zaru. Live now!' the west wind said.

'I know . . . I know,' said Zara.

'Be calm, Zara. Be patient. Do not hurry!' the west wind said, kissing Zara, moistening her face.

'It is essential that you do not break anybody's heart with your words. Do not give. Just love, Zaru!'

And all was quiet again.

Chapter 11

Early in the morning, as the sun rose in the eastern sky, painting the canvas overhead in shades of pink and blue, Zara stood at the edge of the forest, facing a vast mustard field to the west, blanketed by tiny yellow flowers crowning slender green stalks, beyond which flowed the river at a distance in a giant muddy swell of a curve, hugging the field in her gentle sweep, its far bank flanked by a wide glass, steel- and sandstone-clad structure fronting the city of Zara's imagination.

The building basked in the pale-pink reflection of dawn under the great dark void higher up that, in turn, was pierced by the white marble pyramid atop the black granite skyscraper, rising behind the sandstone building, to merge into the light-blue sky enclosing the forest behind Zara in a broad arc.

Zara waved a silent goodbye to the forest. The koel sang in the deep, 'Cooh . . . cooh!'

Zara watched nature's glory unfolding in marvellous rapture, in 360-degree loop from her toe forward, then rising from the horizon as she stood erect, in a trance, her arms resting at her waist, her hips drawn in, her chest drawn out. And she drew in a deep breath, drowning her senses in the breeze made fragrant by the scent of the dry earth beneath her feet.

'Just observe, Zaru, soak in the beauty of the moment to which you now belong, that's knowledge,' the west wind whispered, caressing her face, hugging Zara tight, and planting a soft moist kiss on her cheek.

Zara shut her eyes, stood silently, listening.

And then, she said in a husky voice, 'The forest is gone.'

'The forest is still there where it was, Zaru,' the west wind retorted, 'it's you who has left the forest behind to reach your destination. It had nothing to do with you.'

And the west wind rose to the sky.

'Go, make yourself, Zaru,' she said, 'but be careful not to make others. The thirsty shall seek their own wells of wisdom.'

'I get it. So, how do I make myself from now on?' shouted Zara, looking skywards.

'It's easy, darling,' the west wind said, turning her face to the ground where Zara stood. 'Let me tell you the dos and don'ts of being.'

'To be myself?' Zara asked.

'Yes,' said the west wind. 'Don't seek advice in place of practice. Don't seek company in place of solitude. Don't seek to construct in the midst of destruction. Seek not when it's time to give up.'

'Practice to walk alone and deconstruct the labyrinth of your mind in order to rid yourself of fear,' interrupted Zara.

'Yes, well said, Zaru. That's how you will reach your destination,' the west wind said, rising higher and higher.

Zara waved at the west wind . . . reflecting and thinking.

Thinking!

And she broke into a verse:

High hopes, desperate moments,
Excruciating effort.

The destination far too distant:

A lofty wonder,
Towering above all else
In grand eloquence.

Foreboding, majestic, dark, dominating.
Surveying the creatures below.
Out of the reach of the ordinary,
Yet, captivating
The explorer's imagination,
I wish I could climb!

Hazardous, unscalable peak,
Bewildering!
But, not quite insurmountable.
I'm on the long, narrow path to greatness,
The weak of heart
Curiously milling around . . .

Letting the world know . . .
The journeyman's set his course

In quest for everlasting glory,
Trekking alone through
The dark and dangerous
Bends of the mind.

Steep narrow stairway,
Slippery landings, dark passageways,
And suddenly, a monstrous abyss
Interrupting the path.
A shrill cry piercing the ear . . .
I wish to run back to where I belong.

And then, there's stillness
Quiet!
The summit right ahead,
Standing proud,
Still unconquered.
But now, I know . . .

I have arrived!
Calmness manifest,
That's I.
Countless arms rising high:

'Om Shanti!'

In unbounded joy, I find completion.

Chapter 12

'Welcome to your Universe, Zara,' a voice called out from yonder, far beyond the mustard field, at a distance of an elephant's day-long march, where the river flowed by in glorious majesty.

Zara looked up, stretched out her arms to the world, and smiled.

And then, she stepped out into the field, one foot forward, twirling in the breeze. Twirling . . . twirling . . . twirling . . . when, all of a sudden, the west wind came down on her in one giant swoop, wrapping herself around Zara in a tight embrace in clockwork motion, first, gently and then, gathering pace with the force of a gale. And the earth at her feet merged with the mustard yellow and green, with the muddy brown of the river, with the dazzle and glitter of the steel and glass and sandstone and dark granite, with the blue of the sky above, with the hues of the rainbow, stretching into a sea of white, before eventually plunging into the dark ocean of a full-blown tornado, heartlessly cold, uprooting Zara from the ground and tossing her heavenwards.

And in that churning, Zara started losing control of her sense of self, rapidly shedding height from a staff long, four arms in length, to an arm's measure, to a foot long, to fourteen times smaller, the size of a thumb, to ten times still smaller, the size of a barley corn, to that of a mustard seed, to the point of a human hair, shrinking further to a particle of dust, where she ceased to exist in visible light, to ten nanometres in size, and then, down to an atom, super condensing at 454 degrees below zero Fahrenheit, where she began to lose control of her senses, mind, intellect, and ego. There, her eyes could not see, her mind could not grasp, her deathless self had neither colour nor creed, neither eyes nor ears, neither hands nor feet nor mouth.

And so, in the flutter of an eyelid, Zara was reduced to Z.E.R.O., at which point, she let out a primordial scream: 'I aaaaaaaaaam Nothing!'

And that, indeed, was the moment when her self became infinite in the great, and in the small, everlasting and changeless, the source of life, unborn, without the body and mind.

And her voice, trapped in the monster whirlwind, resonated, 'Nothing . . . nothing . . . nothing . . . othing . . . a thing . . . a thing . . . a Thing . . .'

And even as the echo drowned, a deep sonorous voice emerged from within the hollow of the gale:

'Where there is Nothing, Zara, there is always Something.'

And with that, the whirlwind unfurled in rapid anti-clockwise motion, unwinding Zara at the speed of thought.

And Zara heard the voice of darkness say:

From Nothing arises Consciousness . . .
That arousal is Movement
This Movement is Reverberation
That Reverberation is Energy
This Energy is Power
That Power is the Basis of Attraction
This Attraction is the Basis of all Creation
That Creation is the Reverberation of Something
That appears as Nothing
This Nothing is the Whole
That Whole is symbolised by the Dot
(Whereupon Zara reappeared in visible light within the funnel of the whirlwind to the point of a particle of dust, blue in colour spinning on its own axis.)
This Dot is the manifestation of Nothing
That, indeed, is the Self that is Centred on and Complete in Itself
This Dot that appears as Nothing is Virtual Reality
The Consciousness of this Dot, which is the Self, is Self-Consciousness
That Self-Consciousness is the Ego
This Ego is Mine
That that is Mine belongs to Me
This Me is what the Self perceives of Me
That that the Self perceives of Me Within is what the Self sees of Me.
This Self indeed is that Self
That Self sees this Self with the Eye
This Eye sees that Self with the Inner Eye
That Inner Eye is I

This I is the Quantification of Zero
That Quantification is also the first known Quantity
This Quantity of I is an Idea
(Whereupon a second Dot appeared in the dim light of the funnel, green in colour, each dot now the size of a point of a hair, spinning on its own axis and orbiting one another.)
That Idea is the Eternal Nature of I
This Nature in its Original State is Instinct
That Instinct leads to Individuality
This Individuality results in Identity
That Identity creates the Image
This Image is the Icon
That Icon leads to You
This You is Universal
That Universal is Knowledge
This Knowledge of I resides in You
That Knowledge is what I Need
This Need is what IOU
That that IOU is the Trinity of Being
This Trinity is represented by this I, in my original state of being that resides in what appears as nothing that reverberates as the Idea of individuality that gives me the identity that creates the image that is the icon that is You that is Complete in itself
Therefore, IOU in the culmination of the Self in You
That indeed is the Beginning and this also is the End

This is the Spirit that created the Son out of the Father
That Spirit is the Basis of Faith
This is Therefore That
That Therefore is I Am
This I Am is what You are
That Therefore, is what IOU
That that IOU is the culmination of this Self in that You, making for a Virtuous Circle
(Upon which the two Dots were joined by Zara's Image as a third Dot, red in colour, each dot now the size of a mustard seed spinning on its own axis and orbiting one another in a virtuous circle within the funnel.)
This Circle reverberates into bigger and bigger circles centred on the Dot
That Dot is I
This Circle is, therefore, the Reverberation of the I in You
That IOU is the manifestation of the Idea that is I, and that Idea is Nothing, rendering Myself Zero till it becomes You
This You is only a Virtual Manifestation of that I manifested in the Idea
That You cannot be proven otherwise but for the Real I that by itself appears as Nothing
This is also to say in Real, IOU Nothing
That, indeed, is the basis of Transaction
This is also to say that that Real is Void
That is also to say that that Virtual, too, is Void

This is to say that in Virtual Reality what appears to be Real is also Virtual
That is to say that as in the Real, so in Virtual Reality, IOU Nothing
This is to say that when IOU Nothing, I am Free
This Freedom, therefore, is Virtual Reality
That Freedom is also Real because this Me that is Virtual is also that Me that is Real
This is because I cannot exist in reality just by Myself and need to Create You, that is virtual Me
That is the reason that I need to live in Virtual Reality
This makes Me live in You
That alone, Therefore, is the Basis of Relationship
This Relationship is the first Virtuous Cycle that grows out of I in You and encompasses the Universe in larger and larger Reverberations from Family to Community to Society to Nation to Commonwealth to Planet to the Solar System to the Galaxy to the Universe to the Cosmos
(And with that, the funnel formed by the whirlwind began to disintegrate, refracting into the colours of the rainbow.)
That really is the Game
And in this Game, IOU Nothing
Therefore, there is no this Winner and that Loser
This Game is Tied and
That Tie is Love All.

'That, Zaru, is the essence of life,' the west wind whispered as Zara began to regain control of herself.

Level IV

The Song of Creation Revisited

Chapter I

It was late afternoon in early autumn. The Libra sun shone upon the ageless river, forming golden ripples over its dark and expansive surface.

On its western bank, rose the city of Zara's imagination, a day's sail away from where the river merged languidly with the south sea.

Nine broad steps in alternating pink and black fluorescent glass ascended from the river to a promenade paved with polished black granite, at the far end of which stood a mile-wide low-rise pink glass and steel building, fronted by a row of shop windows, its facade embellished with slabs of hand-hewn soft pink sandstone sculptures. A blue neon sign scrawled across the top of the facade read: 'Ah!nandita Hills'.

Two tall tin soldiers, named Thunder and Bolt, in peacock blue jackets—braided in gold—and shiny green gendarmerie hats pinned with gem-studded butterfly insignia, stood guard at the main entrance to the Ah!nandita Hills, leading to a long and narrow mirrored discotheque, atop which was scrawled a graffiti: 'Greater the challenge, greater the excitement!'

At the far right of the promenade, stood a giant banyan in isolated splendour, in the radiance of its illuminating green leaves and translucent hanging roots. A solitary green bird with red eyes sat staring at a lonely blue bird, perched a short distance away, eyeing bright red figs among the leaves. Members of the Rivah!bank Philharmonic Orchestra—instruments in hand, in panama hats, off-white trousers, white shirts and fawn jackets with matching bow ties and gold lapel pins designed as tittiri birds, led by the redoubtable Zubin Em—milled around two ballerinas, one in a white frock and the other in black, serenading each other below the tree to the accompaniment of the didgeridoo, blown by a short dark man in a red loin cloth and curly white hair, practising for the evening's rendition of the Swan Lake.

The fragrance of a thousand different flowers enveloped the air. Two pretty damsels in floral-print tunics sat on the promenade in front of a florist, embroidering elaborate finery on spreads of hand-woven pashmina.

Not far away, the wicked Kathakali dancer in silk robe and tall golden crown sat on a wooden bench in front of a beauty parlour, busy painting his face green, next to the hollow man, a mustachioed magician, face painted white, rolling a turban over his head.

At the opposite end from the banyan to the extreme left, a matron, in a neon-green Lacoste tee and canary-yellow Crocs, stood at the head of five hundred animated acrobats from Cirque du Soleil in canary-yellow Lacoste tees and neon-green Crocs. Below, a banner of the musical *Wicked* rolled down the building's glass facade.

A patisserie, a tea shop, a bookstore, an art gallery, a fashion studio, a perfumery, and a jeweller's nest sat tidily, one after another, alongside the florist and the beauty parlour.

A slender skyscraper, clad in polished black granite and topped by a pyramid of white Italian marble piercing the soft blue sky, fused with the mirrored discotheque, stood behind the Ah!nandita Hills. Neat white alphabets etched on the river face of the high-rise read: 'Moonshine Mount'.

The city of nine gates, abounding in clean water and fresh air, spread out behind the skyscraper in a succession of seven semi-circular grids of single-storeyed flat-roofed row houses, alternately painted lime white and indigo blue, interspersed with tanks and gardens, and framed at its extreme far end by the curved red oxbow lake of lust and wrath, beyond which, expanding into the vast and endless horizon, lay the dark and foreboding shanty town, without an exit, blanketed by toxic air, and drowning in muck and sewage.

The city of a million dreams worked by day and revelled by night, housing all the planet's beautiful souls, each a super hero—masterchefs, jewellers, fashion designers, models, sportsmen, sculptors, artists, singers, musicians, actors, playwrights, writers, film-makers, architects, inventors, scientists, philosophers, and, above all, the poets—grounded in prosperity, hovering around in wheel-less self-driving electric cars and drones, breathing unpolluted, rarefied air, and feeding off each other in hope and joy, fame and fortune, celebration and euphoria, bereft of dejection and despair, fear and sorrow, and squalor and agony that marred the lives of the calculating creatures, toiling in filth and grime of their minds' ghetto across the red oxbow lake.

And so, the unvanquished city, unrivalled in sports, performing arts, music, paintings, architecture, literature, science and philosophy, celebrated the wisdom of its inhabitants, boasting a glorious past, celebrating its marvellous present, and hallucinating on a still brighter future.

The city, truly, was Zara's destination. To reach it, she had set out from the riverside at the foot of the mountains on elephant back many, many moons ago.

***

Upriver, at some distance from Ah!nandita Hills, a giant arc of a rainbow descended into the river, piercing through the woolly clouds kissing the heavens above.

And as the sun prepared to take its last bow behind the Moonshine Mount, Zara came rolling rapidly down the rainbow—moving without feet, holding without hands, seeing without eyes, hearing without ears, crouched in a foetal position inside a zorb ball burnished chocolatey brown with a copper sheen.

And thousands upon thousands more zorb balls came rolling down the rainbow in the wake of Zara, with her countless lookalikes crouched in a foetal position, some fair complexioned, others pink, some pale, still others brown, and the rest dark, without feet . . . without hands . . . without eyes . . . without ears.

And Zara, now in full command of her senses, comforting in the warmth of the rainbow, heard the deep sonorous voice that had appeared inside the whirlwind, say:

> The essence of life, Zaru, is to build a relationship by renouncing one's dignity in love.
> This I is complete in its Game
> That Game is complete in its Dignity
> This Dignity is complete in its Worthiness that is Innate to its Identity in the State of Nature
> This Worthiness is awakened by Excellence
> That Excellence is achieved when the Self is One with its Other
> This Oneness is the Basis of Love
> That Love is the Basis of Sharing
> This Sharing leads to Renunciation of the Self in the Other for Common Good
> That Renunciation leads to Division of this Whole, which is the Division of that Self, which is the Division of this Idea, which is the Division of that Identity, which is the Division of this Image, which is the Division of that Excellence, which is the Division of this Love with the Other.
> This Division, in Reality, amounts to Nothing
> That Division, in Virtual Reality, amounts to Division of Everything that makes for Innate Dignity

This Sharing leads to Splitting the Whole in Two,
which then, is no longer One, even when imparted
with exactly the same Attributes in Equal Measure
That Splitting leads to Creation
This Creation leads to Preservation
That Preservation leads to Ownership
This Ownership between Two results from
Ownership of One by the Other . . .
And that, Zara, is the essence of Love.

And even as she heard that voice riding the rainbow, Zara bored a wormhole inside her zorb ball to emerge in the open with a thousand eyes, a thousand feet and a thousand arms growing out of a single torso like tendrils emerging out of the creeper's stalk, wrapping herself around the orb at a space of ten fingers.

And Zara's several lookalikes riding the rainbow, some with seven faces, others with twelve hands, and still others with six feet, too, bored wormholes to emerge in the open and wrap themselves around their respective orbs ten fingers apart.

Before long, the thousands upon thousands of zorbs, led by Zara's, descended into the river, one after another, one upon the other, floating in a multitude of soapy bubbles towards the embankment where the nine broad steps rose to the promenade.

And in that twilight moment, the rainbow split into laser beams in shades of violet, indigo, blue, green, yellow, orange, and red. Each beam piercing a zorb, one at a time, inverting them inside out into transparent tubes hollowed in the centre on which floated Zara and her countless cousins in human forms. Among them, in pairs, came Lee.Na and Bey. Ree, Bob.Ess and Dow.Raa, and in singles, came Boo. Bee and Vik.Tor and Bun.Too and Baa.Boo and Kno. Dee and Baa.Goo and Baa.Bai and Gop.Poo and Sau. Mow and Gar.Gee and Pee.Yush and Prat.Yush and Dee.Yaa and Ree.Kaa and Tan.May and Pee.Koo, along with a billion other lookalikes.

And the river turned into a gigantic water park, rising and falling in one giant gentle tide after another. And the seven colours of the rainbow transformed into colourful waterslides, big and small, rising up and falling into the river in twists and turns and hairpin bends and upside down as adrenaline-pumping roller coasters on which Zara and her cheerfully noisy lookalikes frolicked to the music of the Rivah!bank Orchestra, played to the wave of the wand of Zubin Em in off-white trousers and fawn jacket, accompanied with the didgeridoo, played by the short dark man with curly white hair in red loin cloth, on the steps leading to the promenade where the two ballerinas in black and white frocks circled each other in a death dance centred on the wicked Kathakali dancer, while the flower girls in pashmina shawls showered a thousand petals on them and the hollow man stood behind, silently juggling his white turbaned head with mascara-lined eyes and red smiling lips in thin air, tossing it between this hand and that. And the tall tin soldiers marched in goose-steps from here to there and there to here, while the five hundred animated acrobats led by the matron from the Cirque trooped in, vaulting and somersaulting all over the promenade, synchronising every step with the band's symphony, in harmony with a row of dancing fountains, under the glare of arc lights and laser beams that turned the riverbank into an extravagant open-air theatre under a star-spangled sky.

Chapter 2

As the full moon rose atop the Moonshine Mount in the ecstasy of the light-and-sound spectacle on the promenade, Zara paddled her tube towards the nine steps, upon which was rolled out a long red carpet all the way up to the promenade and beyond the entrance of the long-mirrored disco guarded by the two tin soldiers. And following her, Zara's countless cousins, too, paddled their tubes towards the riverbank.

There, alighting on the first step with her companions chanting, 'Hu va, hu va, hu va!' in rapturous applause of the performers, Zara, twenty-four years old and five feet seven inches tall, stood resplendent in an off-white Versace cashmere tunic, a pair of orange Christian Louboutin stilettos with broad wrap-around butterfly ankle ties, matching ochre Hermes scarf and belt with a frog buckle with topaz eyes set in rose gold, an emerald- and ruby-studded lizard broach enamelled green by Van Cleef & Arpels, and a diamond-studded elephant bracelet by Cartier with a matching ring set in white gold. A small red dot, the size of a drop of blood, sat prettily between her eyebrows.

'Where did I come from?' Zara asked.

'You come from yourself, Zara,' said the river in celebration.

'But how did I come here?' Zara wondered aloud, climbing to the step above.

'You came here riding time, Zara. Time, indeed, is your father,' said the river.

'Time? Fathah? And how did I come here riding time?' Zara asked, climbing one more step.

'Your desire of you rode time here,' said the river.

'And how did that happen?' asked Zara, climbing yet another step.

'Remember those words inside the whirlwind when you cried out that you had become nothing?' the river asked.

Zara was silent. She had no recollection of that moment.

'Those words were your desire to become something that expanded in time,' the river said as Zara climbed up one more step.

'Your desire illumined your senses with the colours of the rainbow, Zara, so that you could reach out to your higher self within, just as the tendrils of the plant reach out for sunlight. And that light generated heat. And that heat created the germ of life in you that we call the seed. And that seed is what you ceded of yourself within you, splitting you into two. And the seed that you spilt from you, split into two—one black and one white. And each of those two seeds split thrice over into a pair of seeds each—three pairs black and three pairs white. And each of those twelve seeds split into two, either black or white. And each of those black or white seeds split into two, either black or white. And each of those seeds split into two pairs of seven seeds each, either black or white. And each of those seven seeds split into two, either black or white. And each of those black or white seeds split into two, either black or white. And each of those seeds further split into two, either black or white, and each of those seeds split into two, either black or white, whereupon each of those seeds split into fifteen seeds, either black or white. And each of those black or white seeds split into two, either black or white. And one of those seeds that split from you, Zara, has now become you in a multitude of your likeness that has come along with you riding the rainbow to my bank.'

'That's also how one became many, Zara,' continued the river.

'What then, is time?' Zara asked, rising yet one more step.

'Time is the distance you covered for the idea of you to become you and, therefore, turn full circle,' said the river.

'And how does one come full circle?' Zara asked, rising up to the seventh step.

'Time rides light that reflects itself to come full circle,' said the river, adding, 'just like the sun reflected in the pool on my dry bed many, many moons ago, when you came crashing out of your bubble on the wedge on the river bed between the Moonshine Mount and the Chariot Ridge, Zara.'

'And how does light travel?' Zara asked on the penultimate step before stepping on the promenade.

'Light travels from absolute darkness to bright light to big dazzle, Zara, before reducing to dim light and returning to absolute darkness. The period from complete darkness to big dazzle makes one half of the journey, and the period from big dazzle to complete darkness makes the other half. And each of those halves split thrice over, in a pair of two equal measures, each pair reflecting a mood or season—three pairs dark and gloomy, three bright and sunny. And each of those seasons split into two halves, each called a month. And each of those months split into two, each called a fortnight. And each of those fortnights split into two, each called a week. And each of those weeks split into seven, each in several shades of the sun. And each of those seven split into two, one dark and one bright, called night and day. And each of those days and nights split into two halves, each half of six moods, each mood defined as an hour. And each of those hours split into two halves, each a period in time. And each period split into two, each a moment, whereupon each moment split into fifteen equal parts, each a second. And each second split into two parts, each a flutter. And that flutter is the time you took, Zara, to ride the whirlwind to my bank from the edge of the forest,' the river said, smiling at Zara.

'And where does this light come from?' asked Zara, nonplussed, climbing up to the promenade.

'That light rests in your eyes, Zara, and it appears and disappears with every flutter of your eyelid.'

And as the river said so, the thousands upon

thousands of the zorbs-turned-tubes on which Zara and her lookalikes came, first rolling down the rainbow and then floating down the river, rose to the sky as lamps, and the sky lit up in a burst of fireworks above the Moonshine Mount under the full moon night as Zara's countless lookalikes climbed the steps in her footsteps.

And the Rivah!bank Orchestra reached a crescendo.

And Zara, calm personified, asked, 'And what moves the eyelids?'

'Warmth moves your eyelids,' said the river.

'And what gives warmth?' Zara asked.

'It's heat that provides warmth,' said the river.

'And what gives heat?' Zara asked.

'Food generates heat, Zara,' said the river.

'Go, walk across the promenade to the entrance of the Ah!nandita Hills, where challenge turns into excitement,' the river exhorted. 'There, inside the mirrored disco, you will meet the hollow man, who sees the unseen, hears the unheard, tastes the untasted, thinks the unthought, and knows the unknown. He, alone, will lead you through nine sliding doors, to a secret chamber deep inside the corridor called 'Mamaroy's Kitchen', painted in the subtlest shades of the lotus. There, you will attain the fulfilment of your desire.'

The river continued, 'Whatever your spirit has longed for all these years is to be found within that small space that is as great as the infinite space beyond. For there, upon a giant oven, dwell the sun and the moon, the lightning and the stars, the fire and the air, and the water. There is no old age, no decay, no withering away, no hunger, no thirst. There, you can feast your senses to delight your eyes, playing music to your ears, watering your mouth, rejuvenating your mind, and feeding your soul to warm your body to move on, Zara,' said the river.

Zara didn't take long to walk the red carpet to the entrance of the Ah!nandita Hills, where she came face-to-face with the two tin soldiers—Thunder and Bolt—guarding the entrance to the disco.

'Access control?' she asked, smiling.

'Who are you?' asked the soldiers, straight-faced, without blinking.

'Jo tu hai, so main hoon; jo main hoon, so tu hai,' smiled Zara.

'About turn,' commanded the soldiers. 'Access denied.'

Zara turned around towards the river, and found neither the river nor the performers, nor her lookalikes who had been following her down the rainbow to the now empty promenade. Instead, a dark and deserted embankment descended into nine slippery steps at the edge of the world.'

Zara turned around hurriedly to face the tin soldiers once more and demand the right of passage.

'By what did you acquire your strength to reach here?' asked Thunder.

'By breath,' replied Zara.

'By what did acquire your form?' asked Bolt.

'By eyes,' replied Zara.

'By what did you acquire your voice?' asked Thunder.

'By ears,' replied Zara.

'By what did you acquire your odour?' asked Bolt.

'By nose,' replied Zara.

'By what did you acquire the flavours?' asked Thunder.

'By tongue,' said Zara.

'By what did you acquire your movement?' asked Bolt.

'By feet,' said Zara.

'By what did you acquire your actions?' asked Thunder.

'By hands,' said Zara.

'By what did you acquire your pleasure and pain?' asked Bolt.

'By body,' said Zara.

'By what did you acquire your identity?' asked Thunder.

'By mind,' said Zara.

'By what did you acquire your judgment of right or wrong?' asked Bolt.

'By intelligence,' replied Zara.

And with that, the soldiers stepped aside and the first of the nine glass doors slid apart, revealing the first boxed compartment of a long, narrow-mirrored corridor partitioned at regular intervals.

Chapter 3

Zara stepped into the corridor to be greeted by her million reflections in skin-fit leggings and miniskirts and hot pants paired with matching tank tops and off shoulders from across mirrored walls of the discotheque, dancing in the flash of strobe lights in step with the moonwalking magician, hollow head in hand, and to the ear-blasting music of Mykul Jay's *Eat it*!

They told her don't you ever come around here
Don't want to see your face, you better disappear
The fire's in their eyes and their words are really clear
So eat it, just eat it
You better run, you better do what you can
Don't want to see no blood, don't be a pretty girl
You want to be a beauty, better do what you can
So eat it, but you want to be smart
Just eat it, eat it, eat it, eat it
No one wants to go hungry
Showin' how funky and elegant is your flight
It doesn't matter who's wrong or right
Just eat it, eat it
Just eat it, eat it

Just eat it, eat it
Just eat it, eat it
They're out to get you, better live while you can
Don't want to be a girl, you want to be a woman
You want to stay alive, better do what you can
So eat it, just eat it . . .

'But your song is not what I desire to understand,' yelled Zara above the din of the disco, striding down the corridor.

'But you should know the singer,' said the hollow man walking backwards, facing Zara.

And so, the second door slid open and in walked Zara into the next mirrored compartment in the invisible footsteps of the magician. And the music grew louder:

You better run, you better do what you can
Don't want to see no blood, don't be a pretty girl
You want to be a beauty, better do what you can
So eat it, but you want to be smart
Just eat it, eat it, eat it, eat it . . .

And Zara's million reflections danced in jubilation.

'But your music is not what I desire to understand,' yelled Zara, reaching the end of the second compartment.

'But you should know the musician,' said the hollow man, before the third glass door slid open, making way for the two to step into the next compartment, where the music grew even louder:

> No one wants to go hungry
> Showin' how funky and elegant is your flight
> It doesn't matter who's wrong or right
> Just eat it, eat it
> Just eat it, eat it
> Just eat it, eat it
> Just eat it, eat it . . .

And Zara's countless reflections twirled in gay abandon.

'But your dance is not what I desire to understand,' shouted Zara.

'But you should know the dancer,' the hollow man shouted back, as the fourth glass door parted open, and the music grew still more louder:

> They're out to get you, better live while you can
> Don't want to be a girl, you want to be a woman
> You want to stay alive, better do what you can
> So eat it, just eat it . . .

And Zara's reflections worked up the tempo.

'But your form is not what I seek to understand,' shouted Zara.

'But you should understand the seer of the form,' the hollow man shouted back. And the fifth door opened and in walked he with Zara in tow. And the music grew wilder:

> They told her don't you ever come around here
> Don't want to see your face, you better disappear
> The fire's in their eyes and their words are really
> clear
> So eat it, just eat it
> Just eat it, eat it
> Just eat it, eat it
> Just eat it, eat it
> Just eat it, eat it . . .

'But your pleasure and pain is not what I seek to understand,' hollered Zara.

'But you should know the discerner of pleasure and pain,' cried the hollow man, dancing backwards. And the sixth door parted, making way for the two to the next compartment, Zara in step with the hollow man. And the music grew still louder:

> They're out to get you, better live while you can
> Don't want to be a girl, you want to be a woman
> You want to stay alive, better do what you can
> So eat it, just eat it . . .

And Zara's many reflections gyrated in tandem.

'But your mind is not what I seek to understand,' Zara shouted.

'But you should know the thinker,' said the hollow man. And with that, the doors opened to the seventh compartment, whereupon a heady aroma of a thousand dishes wafted into Zara's nostrils as the music peaked:

> No one wants to go hungry
> Showin' how funky and elegant is your flight
> It doesn't matter who's wrong or right . . .

'But odour is not what I seek to understand,' screamed Zara.

'But you should know the one that smells the odour,' said the hollow man, turning around to face the eighth glass door that opened into the next compartment. And Zara followed in to face her million reflections jumping in ecstatic frenzy:

> Just eat it, eat it
> Just eat it, eat it
> Just eat it, eat it
> Just eat it, eat it . . .

'But taste of food is not what I seek to understand,' yelled Zara at the top of her voice.

'But you should know the discerner of taste,' cried the hollow man before disappearing with a bang, whereupon the lights went off and the reflections drowned in the hollowness of the hollow corridor and the ninth door parted open . . .

And Zara stood right inside Mamaroy's Kitchen.

Chapter 4

'Where am I?' Zara asked, looking around the oval room, astounded. Slender petals rose to the ceiling in broad brushstrokes of soft ceramic pink that gradually merged into the unfolding shades of porcelain white, giving the feel of a lotus in full bloom under a domed ceiling plastered with ceramic tiles periodically changing hues from softer to darker shades of the blue sky—glazed in the pottery barns of Samarkand—from which hung slender pink and white porcelain chandeliers with slender green stems handcrafted at Lladro's workshop in Valencia; the floor tiled at uneven levels with large round ceramic pottery fired into green lotus leaves at Arabia's Helsinki studio, on which stood nine delicate tables with round pietra dura tops designed at the marble workshops of Agra, each surrounded by five crystal chairs, representing the five senses of sound, sight, smell, touch, and taste, with pink backrests and green legs sculpted into shape at Swarovski's workshop in Wattens. A large round steel Gaggenau flatbed charcoal oven laden with Le Creuset pots and pans from Fresnoy-le-Grand hummed with life under an equally large round steel Elica chimney from Fabriano in the centre of the room.

'This is the infinite space of your heart, Zara, the dwelling of your soul. It is free from hunger, free from thirst, free from old age, free from death, and free from grief,' Zara heard a husky feminine voice from across the oven.

Looking up, she saw a beautiful middle-aged porcelain-complexioned, bright-eyed, full-bosomed lady with ample bottom, warmth oozing from her delicate rose-tinted face with lips painted coral and crowned with silken hair in cool auburn undertones, trimmed bouncy to her shoulders, staring from behind the steaming pots over the slow burning charcoal fire, love flowing freely from her heart.

'Who are you?' Zara asked, walking towards the oven.

'I am the real me,' said the lady, 'but they call me Nigella El. I am also known as Mamaroy!'

'And what is the real you?' asked Zara, narrowing her eyes.

'The senses that brought you here are all true. And the one who lives the truth is the real. And I am the one who lives the senses. So, all this that is served here in my kitchen to please your senses is also real. All this is you, too,' said Nigella.

'And what's this?' Zara asked, pointing to the glowing fire spread out on the oven.

'This is the world of fire, Zara. The heat that shines in your eyes, that hums in your ears, that wafts through your nose, that waters your mouth and fires your passion is equalised in the fire of this hearth, consuming the food and arousing the senses that toss your mind up and down the chute of your imagination,' said Nigella.

'Food? And what's this food?' asked Zara, peeping into the pots and pans.

'Ah food! Well, I am food! I am food, I am food; I am the devourer of food! I am the devourer of food, I am the devourer of food,' said Nigella.

'Food, Zara, is the highest state of being,' she went on, 'for truly life is food.'

'When you are starved of food, you cease to feel, you cease to smell, you cease to hear, you cease to touch, you cease to speak, you cease to see, you cease to think, you cease to be.'

'And when you do get to eat, life blooms in you. And you begin to think, you begin to speak, you begin to see, you begin to touch, you begin to hear, you begin to smell, you begin to feel, Zara.'

'All creatures that you saw by the riverbank, a little while ago, and in the forest and at the foot of the mountains on your way here, run about day after day, desiring food. The sun feeds on its own light and gives forth heat, so does the fire that feeds on wood to blaze. And so do you and me. Truly, this Universe was born with the desire for food.'

'From food are creatures, that dwell on earth, produced; by food they live and again into it, they finally pass.'

And saying so, Nigella El thrust a tab into Zara's hands. And so, as Zara swiped the screen with her finger, she saw the everlasting feast of life laid out on the screen, now simmering on the oven.

Appetisers

Golden Ostera Caviar
Caramelised Onion Soup: Served with Gruyere and Parmesan cheese and crouton

Zara was only beginning to grasp what was on offer when Nigella interrupted her, peeling an onion: 'Don't get taken up by the broth, Zara. When you peel an onion to its end, you are only left with its essence. That essence alone is you. When you feel the essence, you absorb everything. Your name and identity are only your skins. Sometimes they grow and sometimes they shrink. It's only when you peel the skins, that you reach your essence. And from that essence another onion is born. So, feel the essence of your soul, Zara.'

Zara looked at her, then at the steaming pots and pans before withdrawing to the tablet in her hand. In a while, her face stiffened as her jaw dropped in horror.

There was a veritable fare for the main course. Would she like it?

Entrée

Eggs Benedict: Peacock eggs with grilled asparagus, house-cured salmon, and home fries
Koel Confit: Slow-cooked koel served with lentils and potato confit

Tongue-tied Bird: Half-roasted tittiri with an apricot glaze served with rice
Frog Barbecue: Grilled frog, brined then basted with hickory barbecue sauce and roasted to fork tender
Mahee Mahee: Mahseer grilled with chimichurri, mango salsa, asparagus, and roasted potatoes
Turtle Roll: One-pound salty game turtle from the edge of the forest served with celery and mayonnaise
Lizard Green Masala: Boiled green monitor lizard served with mint, coriander, and ground spices
Cur-ed Curative: Wild cur in lemongrass, sautéed, served with hot earthworm paste and steamed quinoa
Hungry Hai: Whole roasted rack of spiced hyena served with potatoes gratin, chard cherry tomatoes, and themali plum sauce
Hunter's Delight: Wild boar with onion jam, cooked spelt with saffron
Croc au Pillar: Red-wine braised crocodile short ribs with thick caterpillars tossed in creamy mushroom and black truffle cream sauce
Filet Rhi! Poivre: Broiled rhino tenderloin served with a creamy peppercorn sauce, fries, and seasonal vegetables
Rivah!bank Stripe Steak: Big, juicy, a twenty-eight-day-aged elephant stripe steak seasoned and fire-grilled. Topped with crispy fried grasshoppers

on herb butter and served with mashed potatoes and seasonal vegetables

Virgin Veggie: Grilled vegetable napoleon with fresh green vegetable pie

Cocktails

Dragonfly Bowl Cocktail: Deep-fried dragonfly with Malibu coconut rum, pineapple, and orange juice

Southern Jam: Raw monkey brain mixed with fresh red banyan figs, lemon juice, and vodka sprinkled with a dash of small red ants

Dessert

Lord's Gold au Caviar Parfait: Nougat cream, toasted honey bees, white chocolate sauce sprinkled with glow-worms, and topped with 24-carat gold-coated butterfly

'Slaugh . . . terrrrrrrr!' Zara screamed and the tablet fell from her hand, her face turning purple, tears rolling down her eyes, the sight of all the creatures of her childhood on the riverbank and the forest slaughtered one after another in the red oxbow lake of lust and wrath flashing past her mind. And there went the train of ants on the dry river bed; the caterpillars crawling under the peepul tree beside the earthworms; the glow-worms flying in the dark of the promenade on the left bank of the river, some distance from the Peacock Ridge; the dragon flies, the grasshoppers, the bees, and the butterflies making a buzz at the sight of the approaching river; Froggy and Lizzy on the steps leading to the promenade, rushing past everybody else for the first dip into the water; wise old Mah!seer deep in meditation midstream. And then the monkeys swinging from the branches at the edge of the forest, the wild cur barking lazily under the morning sun in the meadow; the wild boar grunting in the mud; Redeyes, the hyena, in the dark and eerie night of the jungle laughing 'hehehe!'; Rhi!noo, turtle, and Elly? Yes, Elly going down under the pond. And now, all of them swallowed one by one, one after another, in the giant bright orange pots and pans.

'You are killer of life,' Zara shouted at Nigella.

'I am Mamaroy!, giver of life, Zara,' Nigella smiled, her moist coral lips stretched from side to side, warmth oozing from her rose-tinted porcelain face, love pouring out of her heart.

'Know well, Zara,' she said softly, 'Those who kill don't eat; those who eat don't kill.'

'And this, indeed, is the food, that you and I hanker after. So, fear not darling, and hate me not. From food are all these creatures born, by food they grow and live. Because it is eaten by and eats creatures, it is called food. Delight in food, revere your food, as you would revere yourself. All of this creation, to which you belong, is only food and food alone. This fire is the eater of food. This itself is the highest creation.'

And as she said so, blue-white Noritake ceramic tableware with generous servings of Mamaroy!'s choicest dishes floated from the oven to the nine tables spread around the room, their heady aroma wafting in the air, uplifting Zara's senses. And the sparks that blazed in the oven, rose to the chimney.

'As from this blazing fire, a thousand sparks leap forth, so millions of souls are born out of love and return unto it, Zara,' said Nigella. And saying so, she turned a copper pitcher full of water into the oven, raising a giant cloud of steam into the chimney. Then, lifting one foot over the oven, and then the other, she disappeared into the funnel riding the smoke.

Zara peered into the chimney. Then craned her neck to catch one last glimpse of Mamaroy!

Alas! She found no one inside.

Then, as if in a trance, she ascended the oven, one foot at a time, its charcoal bed reduced to dying embers and ashes. And as she did so, she was sucked into the long dark hollow in the blink of an eye.

And she rose up, up, up . . .

And in her wake, the embers rose to the chimney, twinkling like a million stars across a vast swathe of dark emptiness. And so, Zara, in quest for everlasting glory, trekking alone in emptiness through the dark and dangerous bends of the mind, wafted up the steep narrow stairway of Moonshine Mount, past slippery landings and dark passageways, up the chute of her mind. And up, up, up she rose, when in the silence of the deep space of her heart, a shrill cry pierced her ears.

And so, there stood Zara, gloriously perched atop the Moonshine Mount, shining bright in the glow of the full-moon night, under a star-spangled sky.

Zara looked up and looked around and twirled. Raising her hands sideways to shoulder height, she took one small step for the giant leap forward, love pouring out of her heart, words melting in her mouth:

Floating beyond the horizon of reality,
On a carpet of smoke,
I see life abound in joy.
It's a world of goodness, beyond measure.
I leave my world far behind
Flying over the clouds
To a magical place—I find everlasting peace.
As the gateway to knowledge opens
Revealing to me the naked truth . . .
I find my greatest joy
Standing at the golden gate.
There's nothing here, but eternity!
In my flight of fancy
Among the stars, I see no god
Nor another being.
With both my arms outstretched
Grasping the pillars of conviction,
Facing the truth
And nothing, but the truth
I, the eternal being,
The highest form of creation,
Standing all alone by myself
I see none other than me.
The rest, mere projections of that
Great unknown that manifests

As the supreme being in my mind
Ever since I came down to earth.
Rising above the mundane,
I get to understand that
There's only existence.
Existence self-existing.
I, the eternal eye that surveys the world
And pictures myself sometimes
As an elephant, at times as a frog
And yet other times as a lizard, changing colours
And still more often as my likeness,
But another than my own self
Sometimes, I see myself in twos,
At others, in threes, fours; a multitude.
I see myself in you, in you, in you!
Jo tu hai, so main hoon; jo main hoon, so tu hai!
And so, in one and all, I find my whole.

Level V

The End of Story: The Game Begins

Nothing Stirs!

In the beginning, there was a dark, bottomless pit, lonely and silent. The stars of the distant space were shrouded behind the veil of ignorance. Unborn. And in that absolute darkness, darkness crept upon darkness, raising heat. And in that figment of imagination, the first sign of life appeared as the hum of silence. And in that humming, the seed of love was born.

And so, the moments passed by the second as if into minutes and the minutes as if into hours, and the hours as if into days, and the days as if into fortnights, and the fortnights as if into months, and the months as if into years. For, there was no then then, no there there. There was no time. There was no space. When all of a sudden, a flash of lightning tore the darkness, cracking open the wormhole of the mind, splitting the dark space between the earth and the sky.

And into the abyss fell the seed of love, a thousand times smaller than a speck of dust, growing to the size of a tip of hair, growing, growing, growing . . . to the size of a kernel of millet, a mustard seed, a barley grain, a seed of rice, to the size of a bubble. And the bubble grew in the dark and silent hollow, trapping within it the shadows of the earth, the space, the sky, the sun, the moon, the stars, the cosmos. For, the bubble alone was the mind, its body life, its form light, its conception truth, its soul space, containing all desires, all odours, all tastes, encompassing all of creation, without speech, without concern.

And within the bubble, emerged the sonorous voice:

> The Ownership of the I and the Icon leads to Comparison
> This Comparison leads to Desire
> That Desire of the Self is to get back to what originally was
> This Desire then leads to Discontent
> That Discontent leads to Labour
> This Labour leads to Employment
> That Employment leads to Action
> This Action leads to Result
> That Result leads to Envy
> This Envy leads to Anxiety
> That Anxiety leads to Fear
> This Fear leads to Thinking
> That Thinking leads to Passion
> This Passion leads to Lust
> That Lust leads to Enmity
> This Enmity arises when what is split cannot be got back as One without Eliminating the Other
> That Other, if not Eliminated, leads to Hatred
> This Hatred is the opposite of Love
> That Hatred leads to Confrontation
> This Confrontation leads to Violence

That Violence leads to War
This War leads to Destruction
(Upon which the bubble burst and there was darkness once more.)
That Destruction is Liberation
This, then, is the essence of the Universe, trapped within the bubble in a cycle of give and take, of good and bad, fear and hope, joy and sorrow, love and hate, peace and war.
Having travelled beyond the idea of the dot, the self fears dissipation into nothing in the vastness of its reverberations, so it deploys its entire force that emanates out of itself back to the dot that lies at its core within, till it is devoid of energy and is no longer the whole, and so does the identity destroy itself.
This, truly, is the essence of birth and death.
This is also the essence of the collapse of the stars into the wormhole . . .
. . . of the collapse of the worlds . . .
. . . of the collapse of the earth . . .
. . . of the collapse of the plants . . .
. . . of the collapse of the worms . . .
. . . of the collapse of the animals . . .
. . . of the collapse of the forests . . .
. . . of the collapse of habitations . . .
. . . of the collapse of civilisations . . .
. . . of the collapse of philosophies . . .
. . . of the collapse of god . . .
. . . of the collapse of man . . .

And in that complete collapse, life is liberated.
And that life is *sva*. And from that sva pours forth *ha!* the seed of love.
And so, travels light from big dazzle to dim light to absolute darkness . . .
. . . in the hope of a new dawn.

Appendices

The Essence of This and That

In the Beginning there is Something
This Something appears as Nothing
From That Nothing arises Consciousness
This arousal is Movement
That Movement is Reverberation
This Reverberation is Energy
That Energy is Power
This Power is the Basis of Attraction
That Attraction is the Basis of all Creation
This Creation is the Reverberation of Something that appears as Nothing
That Nothing is the Whole
This Whole is symbolised by the Dot
That Dot is the manifestation of Nothing
This indeed is the Self that is Centred on and Complete in Itself
That Dot that appears as Nothing is Virtual Reality
This Consciousness of that Dot, which is the Self, is Self-consciousness
That Self-consciousness is the Ego
This Ego is Mine
That that is Mine belongs to Me
This Me is what the Self perceives of Me

That that the Self perceives of Me Within is what the Self sees of Me

This Self indeed is that Self

That Self sees this Self with the Eye

This Eye sees that Self with the Inner Eye

That Inner Eye is I

This I is the Quantification of Zero

That Quantification is also the first known Quantity

This Quantity of I is an Idea

That Idea is the Eternal Nature of I

This Nature in its Original State is Instinct

That Instinct leads to Individuality

This Individuality results in Indentity

That Indentity creates the Image

This Image is the Icon

That Icon leads to You

This You is Universal

That Universal is Knowledge

This Knowledge of I resides in You

That Knowledge is what I Need

This Need is what IOU

That that IOU is the Trinity of Being

This Trinity is represented by this I in my original state of Being that resides in what appears as Nothing that

Reverberates as the Idea of Individuality that gives me the Identity that creates the Image that is the Icon that is You that is Complete in Itself

Therefore, IOU the culmination of the Self in You

That indeed is the Beginning, and this also is the End
This is the Spirit that created the Son out of the Father
That Spirit is the Basis of Faith
This is Therefore That
That Therefore is I AM
This I am is what You are
That Therefore is what IOU
That that IOU is the culmination of this Self in that You, making for a Virtuous Circle
This Circle reverberates into bigger and bigger circles centred on the Dot
That Dot is I
This Circle is Therefore the Reverberation of the I in You
That IOU is the manifestation of the Idea that is I, and that
Idea is Nothing, rendering Myself Zero till it becomes You
This You is only a Virtual Manifestation of that I manifested in the Idea
That You cannot be proven otherwise, but for the Real I that by itself appears as Nothing
This is also to say in Real, IOU Nothing
That indeed is the basis of Transaction
This is also to say that that Real is Void
That is also to say that that Virtual too is Void
This is to say that in Virtual Reality what appears to be Real is also Virtual
That is to say as in Real, so in Virtual Reality, IOU Nothing
This is to say that when IOU Nothing, I am Free
This Freedom, therefore, is Virtual Reality

That Freedom is also Real because this Me that is Virtual is also that Me that is Real

This is because I cannot exist in reality just by Myself and need to Create You

That You is the virtual Me

This is reason that I need to live in Virtual Reality

That makes Me live in You

This alone, therefore, is the Basis of Relationship

That Relationship is the first Virtual Cycle that grows out of I in You and encompasses the Universe in larger and larger Reverberations from Family to Community to Society to Nation, to Commonwealth to Planet to the Solar System to the Galaxy to the Universe to the Cosmos

This really is the Game

And in That Game, IOU Nothing

Therefore, there is No this Winner and that Loser

This Game is Tied and

That Tie is Love All

This I is Complete in its Game

That Game is Complete in its Dignity

This Dignity is Complete in its Worthiness that is Innate to its Identity in the State of Nature

This Worthiness is Awakened by Excellence

That Excellence is Achieved when the Self is One with its Other

This Oneness is the Basis of Love

That Love is the Basis of Sharing

This Sharing leads to Renunciation of the Self in the Other for Common Good

That Renunciation leads to Division of this Whole, which is the Division of that Self, which is the Division of this Idea, which is the Division of that Identity, which is the Division of this Image, which is the Division of that Excellence, which is the Division of this Love with the Other

This Division, in Reality, amounts to Nothing

That Division, in Virtual Reality, amounts to Division of Everything that makes for Innate Dignity

This Sharing leads to Splitting the Complete Whole, in Two, which then, is no longer One, even when imparted with exactly the same attributes in Equal Measure

That Splitting leads to Creation

This Creation leads to Preservation

That Preservation leads to Ownership

This Ownership between Two results from Ownership of One by the Other

That Ownership of the I and the Icon leads to Comparison

This Comparison leads to Desire

That Desire of the Self is to get back to what originally was

This Desire then, leads to Disconnect

That Disconnect leads to Labour

This Labour leads to Employment

That Employment leads to Action

This Action leads to Result

That Result leads to Envy

This Envy leads to Anxiety

That Anxiety leads to Fear

This Fear leads to Thinking

That Thinking leads to Passion

This Passion leads to Lust
That Lust leads to Enmity
This Enmity arises when what is Split cannot be got back as One without Eliminating the Other
That Other, if not Eliminated, leads to Hatred
This Hatred is the Opposite of Love
That Hatred leads to Confrontation
This Confrontation leads to Violence
That Violence leads to War
This War leads to Destruction
That Destruction leads to Liberation
This, then, is the essence of the Universe, trapped within a bubble in a cycle of give and take of good and bad, fear and hope, joy and sorrow, love and hate, peace and war.

This Space Is Time

1 atom = 0.0000001 mm

10 atoms = 0.000001 mm = 1 nm (nanometre)

100 nm = 1 particle of dust = 0.0001 mm (which is the tiniest visible object of the human eye)

10 particles of dust = 1 point of hair = 0.001 mm

10 particles of hair = 1 kernel of millet = 0.01 mm (0.01 mm is considered to be the tinniest object visible to the human eye)

1 sperm cell = 0.5 mm

10 kernels of millet = 1 seed of mustard = 1.0 mm

10 seeds of mustard = 1 grain of barley = 10 mm = 1 cm (standard contemporary measure of one grain of barley = 8.47 mm)

10 grains of barley = 1 finger = 1.763 cm

14 fingers = 1 ft. = 24.682 cm (the largest standard shoe

size in UK/US is 30.5 cm, which was also derived from the measurement of standard barley corn in the UK)

24 fingers = 1 arm = 42.312 cm

96 fingers = 1 staff = 4 arms = 169.248 cm = 5 ft. 6 41/64 in.

1 staff is also measured as the standard human height.

2,000 staff = distance to which the cow's lowing can be heard = 2,000 x 169.248 cm = 3,38,496 cm = 3,384.96 m = 3.38496 km

4 times the distance of a cow's lowing = 13.53984 km = distance covered by an elephant in a day's march.

1 march of six months = 180 days = time taken for the Sun to move from the South Pole to the North Pole. 180 days is also the time taken by the Sun to move from the North Pole to the South Pole.

360 days* = Distance covered by the Sun from the South Pole to the North Pole and back to the South Pole = 1 year

1 year = 4 seasons of three months each: spring, summer, monsoon, and winter. 1 year is also equal to six seasons of two months each: spring, summer, monsoon, autumn, winter, deep winter.

* Standardised for equal division of year into two halves

1 month = 2 fortnights (new moon to full moon and full moon to new moon) each of 14 days = 28 days

1 fortnight = 7 days

1 day = 1 dark half + 1 bright half = 24 hours = 1,440 minutes = 86,400 seconds

1 bright half = 12 hours

1 hour = 60 minutes = 2 periods

1 period = 30 minutes

1 minute = 30 seconds = 2 moments

1 moment = 15 seconds

1 second = 2 flutters

1 flutter = 1 wink = 0.33 seconds

End Note

Dear Zara,

Thank you for your patience. I hope you found Zara's journey interesting.

I am sure you might be wondering what really happens to Zara later on. Why does the story not provide a closure to Zara? This makes it important to remember that this is a book *for* you, not *about* you.

So, let me revert to the backstory on how this book was designed.

In imagining this story, I borrowed several concepts from diverse streams, many of which have been detailed in my letter to you at the beginning of this book. In crafting *Zara's Witness*, I also looked at the principles of hallucinations and dreams.

You might have already observed that the story unfolds in a series of hallucinations at different levels. Now, the thing about hallucinations and dreams is that they actually do not have a beginning or an end. You always wake up in the middle of a hallucination or, to put it simply, your dream is almost always broken without an ending or a conclusion. That is why dreams are always open to interpretation.

The other thing about dreams is that they take you through parallel terrain that always seems to be familiar ground but is often a place you might not have actually visited before. So, Zara of this book, too, travels from stark wilderness by the riverside, through the forest, to her destination in the city, where she confronts her lookalikes for the first time ever, all alone, before merging with everything in the sky—the other realm of imagination.

There were other thoughts as well, that went into plotting Zara's journey.

We have been taught from childhood about the four stages of life as per ancient Indic wisdom: the *Brahmacharya Ashrama*, the *Grihastha Ashrama*, the *Vanaprastha Ashrama*, and, finally, the *Sannyasa Ashrama*.

Zara's Witness reverses that order starting with the Sannyasa Ashrama by the riverbank where she is mesmerised by evocative memories of her bubble taking shape alongside a multitude of identical bubbles at the tongue of the glacier, high above in the mountains; the Vanaprastha Ashrama that forces her to walk through the jungle and confront personal loss in the death of her long-time companion, Elly, the elephant; and the Grihastha Ashrama, where she reaches the city to find abundance and fulfilment, taking in the sights and senses of soul-enriching food at Mamaroy's Kitchen, which, to borrow Upanishadic thinking, is the very purpose and culmination of all life—we are all part of the great food chain of the Universe. The oven at Mamaroy's Kitchen is the sacrificial pit, the *havan kund* or the *yagna* altar, that transports oblations from mortals on earth to the immortals in the sky.

I felt that Zara's journey to the sky (to the high heavens, as it were) and what happens thereafter, should be left as an open-ended happily ever after rather than forcing a closure. Leaving Zara in the sky is to leave her both at the mercy and/or in the celebration of the readers' imagination. There were three issues here.

First, a deeply emotional one: Zara, as you know, is also you, my daughter. Having given you a peep into your own dormant consciousness about the very nature of your being through the question of 'who am I?' and a hint of what's that big deal about, I was rather uncomfortable giving Zara, the Witness, a closure of any sort. Hence, I avoided the call of logic. I also thought, having told you the story, it would be best to leave you alone to reach your own conclusion in real life: what you should wish to do after hearing it all should really be your business. Twenty-four is a good age to decide where do you wish to go from here, without parental handholding.

Secondly, the nature of Indic philosophy not only spirals upwards, i.e., it ascends from one story to another, but it is also essentially recursive. Which is to say, it is never-ending and almost amounts to the same thing being told over and over again through shifts in the storytelling from generation to generation, from one millennium to another. In a sense, there is actually no ending, no conclusion. The storyteller and the story can go on and on. *Zara's Witness* is just another way-station saga along that stream of everlasting consciousness, recalibrated for your generation, Gen Z.

It could well be that Zara will re-emerge in the intergalactic space at another time, in another journey, in another form en route to another planet, in another galaxy, far, far away. Which makes it necessary to leave Zara with an open-ended plan.

That brings us to reason three, the most significant aspect of Indic wisdom. It is to be found in the concept of *mukti* or *moksha* or *nirvana*. Our seers have long held that by doing good and great deeds alone, it is possible to gain mukti or moksha or nirvana in afterlife, freeing us from the shackles of rebirth. But more importantly, they have also divined that it is possible to gain mukti or moksha or nirvana here and now itself . . . in this very life. Zara's ascent to the sky to discover herself in all and all in her, is symbolic of that mukti or moksha or nirvana. Her salvation could well be here or hereafter. It's for you, Zara, the reader, to decide.

Which is why Level V, the shortest and most abrupt of all the sections, ends with *sva ha!* This is the most sacred sacrificial chant that has prevailed for more than five thousand years. Now sva, which means both the Self and the Sky, has nearly a hundred manifestations, culminating in *svadhin* or freedom or liberation.

That alone must be your ultimate destination, Zara, as it must for Zara, the Witness. And that alone must also be the fodder for another book.

What say, you?

Dad

This fullness is filled with fullness.
Fullness is born from fullness.
Fullness fills fullness.
In fullness, fullness is ever rested.

This collection of poems attempts to unlock the wisdom of our ancient seers for the benefit of the layfolk, often eulogised for their resilience in the face of depredations of time, but with no one to turn to—not even the gods—for succour, mercy, and redemption, and far removed from expensive and time-consuming modern psychiatric intervention. It has nothing to do with religion or rituals; nothing to do with an exclusive or an exclusivist lifestyle. Rather, these poems seek to help us cope with the circumstances that confront us on our eventful walk through life.

In *Shadows of the Fragmented Moon*, each poem has a hidden and unexplored facet of human trait that needs confronting to clear the path of ill-informed illusions. For, as the seers have claimed down the ages, the mind is only an aggregate of desires and nothing else. We humans are a conglomerate of our emotions and reason . . . without purpose, without a second chance.

Understanding this one truth alone sets us free.